# STE. MADELEINE
# COMMUNITY
# WITHOUT
# A TOWN

## METIS ELDERS IN INTERVIEW

### Ken Zeilig

### Victoria Zeilig

PEMMICAN
PUBLICATIONS
INC.

Design by Grandesign Ltd. Winnipeg, Manitoba


Pemmican Publications Inc. gratefully acknowledges the assistance
accorded to its publishing program by
Manitoba Arts Council and Canada Council.


**Printed and Bound in Canada**

---

**Canadian Cataloguing in Publication Data**

Zeilig, Ken, 1939-
   Ste. Madeleine

ISBN 0-919143-45-8

1. Métis—Manitoba—Ste. Madeleine—Social
conditions.* 2. Métis—Manitoba—Ste. Madeleine—
Interviews.* 3. Ste. Madeleine (Man.)—Social
conditions. I. Zeilig, Victoria, 1950- II. Title.

FC113.44 1987      305.8'97'071272      C87-098107-2
E99.M693Z44 1987

---

**PEMMICAN
PUBLICATIONS
INC.**


**411 - 504 Main Street / Winnipeg, Manitoba / Canada  R3B 1B8**

*This book is dedicated to Yvon Dumont, President of the Manitoba Metis Federation, who first told me about Ste. Madeleine and who provided me with the first introductions to the diminishing community of people whose story appears herein.*
*K.S.Z.*

*Later after the story had been recorded, Yvon extended his friendship and time to encourage both authors to see this project through to completion. We trust that his faith in Ste. Madeleine and its people has been rewarded with this modest effort.*
*K.S.Z. and V.R.Z.*

# ACKNOWLEDGEMENTS

We first wish to acknowledge the five Metis people who have so kindly offered their time and wisdom in making this book their own: Joe Venne, Agnes Boucher, Louis Pelletier, Harry Pelletier and Lena Fleury.

Particular thanks go to Joe Venne for his unusual candor and for his enormous patience and enthusiasm in assisting us. Every person with whom we have spoken, from the community of Ste. Madeleine, has been unique and special. But Joe Venne never ceases to amaze us with his remarkable memory and thoughtfulness. We consider ourselves lucky to have him as a friend.

Next, we wish to thank Lazare Fouillard for his great warmth and honesty in offering an outsider's point of view. We also want to acknowledge Lazare and his wife, Rhea, for their splendid hospitality, during the last summer days of September 1987.

And to Thomas Berger, thank you for providing your precise and insightful historical and legal perspective.

Acknowledgements also go to the following people for all their assistance along the way: Yvon Dumont; Ron Erickson; Billyjo DeLaRonde; George Pelletier (son of Harry); George Ducharme; Fred and Yvonne LeClerc and their son, Richard; Josephine Vermette; Leonard Venne (Joe Venne's son) of Regina, Saskatchewan; and Olive Landriault (Joe Venne's daughter) of Timmons, Ontario; Helene Fouillard Huybrecht, especially for her fine translating help; and Father Roger Blondeel of the Parish of St. Lazare.

Thanks go to those special map experts: Dave Perry, Gerry Holm and Jack Mercredi at the Manitoba Department of Natural Resources; and to all the helpful people at the Manitoba Provincial Archives.

Finally, we wish to thank Monsignor Ward Jamieson of the Roman Catholic Archdiocese of Winnipeg for his unique insight and absorbing scholarship.

# CONTENTS

PREFACE . . . . . . . . . . . . . . . . . . . . . . . . . . . . . . . . . . . . . . . . . . . . . . *viii*

INTRODUCTION . . . . . . . . . . . . . . . . . . . . . . . . . . . . . . . . . . . . . . . . . *x*

JOE VENNE . . . . . . . . . . . . . . . . . . . . . . . . . . . . . . . . . . . . . . . . . .  *14*

AGNES BOUCHER . . . . . . . . . . . . . . . . . . . . . . . . . . . . . . . . .  *80*

LOUIS PELLETIER . . . . . . . . . . . . . . . . . . . . . . . . . . . . . . . . . *104*

HARRY PELLETIER . . . . . . . . . . . . . . . . . . . . . . . . . . . . . . *126*

LENA FLEURY . . . . . . . . . . . . . . . . . . . . . . . . . . . . . . . . . . . *152*

THE STE. MADELEINE CHURCH . . . . . . . . . . . . . . . . . . . . *176*

LAZARE FOUILLARD — An Outsider's Perspective . . . . . . . . *182*

THOMAS BERGER — Legal and Historical Perspective . . . . . . *194*

# PREFACE

The story of Ste. Madeleine as recounted in these pages began in the spring of 1986 when the president of the Manitoba Metis Federation, Yvon Dumont, told me about this community which once flourished in western Manitoba. Mr. Dumont had apparently been told about Ste. Madeleine by friends. The bare bones of his tale were that over 250 Metis homesteaded their land for generations until they were kicked off by government fiat; their homes were burned, their dogs where shot in full view of everyone and they were turned off the land without compensation—scattered to the far reaches of northern Manitoba and Saskatchewan.

When I expressed interest, Mr. Dumont introduced me to some of the people who had lived there. Shortly after our initial visit in April, 1986, I began interviewing some of the former inhabitants. This book is their story; in the old-fashioned sense, I was just the scribe, working with modern tools as a microphone and tape recorder. I was bolstered enormously by Victoria's tireless research, patient transcribing, and constructive criticisms.

As the people spoke, it became apparent that a different story of Ste. Madeleine was emerging from the one which Yvon Dumont had told me about in the early spring. It was essentially the story of a vibrant Metis community, untouched by such modern-day problems as violence, alcoholism, chronic unemployment, suicide, despair about the future or concern about the nuclear fate of this planet. The Ste. Madeleine which we discovered through interview and research was a community preserved like one of those rare insects from the past, in the amber memories of five ex-inhabitants! What emerged was a rich social history of what life was like for a unique group of underprivileged Metis farm labourers. It was the remembrance of things past: a community life where everyone helped each other to survive! And in the process, the people took sustenance from each other, they shared food, music, weddings, birth, illnesses and death. The communal bond went beyond the church, the one-roomed school, the shared fun and games at innocent weekend parties; it had something to do with the land!

Although it was never articulated, the implied bond was homeland. This was where the Metis people could be themselves, away from the back-breaking labour on white farms, menial jobs on the fringes of town society, and ever-present discrimination. As one old-time resident of nearby St. Lazare told me, "They were good servants!" In Ste. Madeleine, though, the people were masters of their own fate; they were subservient to no one; they served themselves.

Not a single one of the interviewees from Ste. Madeleine told his or her story without deep emotion. However, harsh memories from the past did not leave scars of bitterness or feelings of revenge; rather time seemed to have mellowed the people, and in an unlikely way, to have enriched them spiritually. Again and again the people spoke about their land. Ste. Madeleine was always HOME even if a family had been away for three years stooking, scrubbing, or digging for seneca root. Ste. Madeleine was their rock, an immutable island of peace, beauty, and bountifulness in an otherwise unrelenting social landscape.

*Talking to the people of Ste. Madeleine sensitized us to the meaning of homeland: to just what it meant to have a land base for one's people! And this was one of the last in Manitoba: it had ties to the turbulent times of 1885 and we, suspect, earlier.*

*No matter how hard I pressed during my questioning in 1986, none of the interviewees seemed to feel that any ONE person was to blame when they were kicked out of Ste. Madeleine in 1938. There were some grumbles, faithfully recorded within these pages, but what I found was more a collective sense of loss for the hallowed memory of a communtiy life that had been, rather than a vengeful finger pointed at a guilty party.*

*However, that picture changed somewhat in July 1987. And with that change, the focus appeared to return to Yvon Dumont's original story: that the Metis from Ste. Madeleine had somehow been short-changed. Perhaps a people had been bullied and pushed from their homeland.*

*During the summer of 1987, we returned to the vicinity of Ste. Madeleine to do more interviews with the people of the area. The interviews were for an Oral History Project on Ste. Madeleine which we were doing for the Manitoba Provincial government. Quite by chance, we came upon Pioneer Days, a yearly celebration, at Fort Ellice, Manitoba. It was there that we met Lazare Fouillard, among others, from the nearby town of St. Lazare. He is one of the sons of Benoit Fouillard, who was a councillor for the municipality of Ellice in the '30s especially during the period when Ste. Madeleine was being fenced in. I plugged my tape recorder into an electrical outlet attached to a telephone pole in the middle of this usually empty field and I began there, in the mid-day sun, to record an interview with Mr. Fouillard.*

*We felt the interview was sufficiently important to the story of Ste. Madeleine that it should be added to the book, even at the eleventh hour. With very little persuasion, our publisher concurred, and accordingly, an extra chapter was included.*

*This new chapter entitled: An Outsider's Point of View, adds a different point of view to the story of the original five interviewees; what's more, it provides some substance to the intriguing thought that perhaps, the president of the Manitoba Metis Federation was right from the beginning!*

*And who knows, maybe the diminishing number of Metis from Ste. Madeleine will yet live to see their wrongs righted.*

*As this Preface is being composed, independent funding is being put together for a film of this story—soon, we hope, the story of Ste. Madeleine will be as familiar in print and on film as any other important chapter of this country's young history.*

                                                                    *K.S.Z.*

# INTRODUCTION

The community of Ste. Madeleine, Manitoba was settled at the turn of the century by Metis homesteaders, many of whose families originally came from the Red River Settlement near Winnipeg.*

Ste. Madeleine's roots go back to 1880, when the famous French missionary, Father DeCorby, first founded the Catholic mission of St. Lazare, close to the Hudson Bay Company trading post at Fort Ellice. Father DeCorby was renowned for his work among the Indians and Metis and for his facility with Indian lauguages. St. Lazare became a parish in 1895. Seven years later, an auxiliary mission was set up in Ste. Madeleine, effectively placing that community on the map.

There is no formal history of the specific area prior to this time. However, it is clear that the routes travelled by the Metis buffalo hunters, pemmican and fur traders between Manitoba and Saskatchewan crossed over this area of the prairies along the Carlton Trail. The Hudson Bay and Northwest Companies maintained complex networks of supply lines across this whole area from the 17th century onward. And the missionaries set up their churches in close tandem.

So when the Metis of the Red River Valley were forced to abandon their settlement after 1870, it was logical they would choose a familiar area in which to make their new home. Also, many Metis who had settled in Saskatchewan, chose to return to Manitoba, following the Rebellion of 1885.

In April, 1872, the first Dominion Lands Act set down the basic policies regulating free quarter-section homestead grants. Each township was divided into 36 square blocks, called sections, and each section (one mile square) thus contained 640 acres. Even numbered sections would be granted as homesteads, while odd-numbered sections were to be reserved as Railway Lands (later public lands). In addition, Sections 11 and 29 of each township were to be set aside for schools while Sections 8 and 26 were deemed Hudson's Bay Company lands.

To acquire a 160-acre homestead, the applicant had to make an entry in person at the Dominion Lands Office, and pay ten dollars. To earn a patent for the homestead, there was a residence requirement of three years, during which time a house must be built, 30 acres of land must be broken and 20 acres cropped.

---

*Several of the people we spoke with told us that their grandparents had come from such areas as Baie St. Paul, St. Francois Xavier, and St. Norbert, which were among the 24 parishes included in the 1870 federal survey of the Red River area. (These original river lots, of course, would later become a major focus of the Metis land claims issue.)

*The first settlers in Ste. Madeleine obtained quarter sections of land, and although the main concentration of homes was later on about four sections (which also included the school and church), all of the families in the township (Township 18, Range 29) were considered part of the community. About six sections of land east of the Assiniboine River were taken up by the Gambler Indian Reserve. The western boundary of the settlement was the province of Saskatchewan.*

*Although a mission was formally established in 1902, the people of Ste. Madeleine still had to travel thirteen miles on horseback to attend church in St. Lazare. Therefore, in 1913, approximately twelve families completed the building of a log chapel in their own village. From then on, a priest would come once or twice a month from St. Lazare to say mass for the Metis people. In fact, in later years these church services would also attract visitors from surrounding communities. We have included in this book, amongst the photographs, a translation of an original document which describes the humorous albeit trying times surrounding the building of the little church.*

*In 1922, the one-room Belliveau School was built on Section 29. Grades 1 through 8 were taught here, sometimes in French, sometimes in English. After 1940, however, the children of Ste. Madeleine were forced to attend the Gambler School, which was located across the Assiniboine River, in the other corner of the township.*

*From 1915 to 1935, this community of Metis grew and thrived, their numbers increasing to about 250 people. They were basically itinerant labourers who worked for farmers in the surrounding areas. But they always considered Ste. Madeleine, with its log cabins, barns and outbuildings, to be their land base. (Each family had maybe three or four head of cattle, and two horses, at most.)*

*At that time, taxation was such that one had three years to pay back taxes on a homestead. Often, because of their bare subsistence living, it was impossible for the families to pay these taxes. The land was divided and subdivided over the years, among different members of the family. They engaged in only minimum farming on this land, because it was basically scrub pasture, with very sandy soil. But the community was home for these people. And, not only that, Metis from Alberta and Saskatchewan visited family members in Ste. Madeleine, making it a well-known Metis community throughout western Canada.*

*In 1935, the Prairie Farm Rehabilitation Act [PFRA] was passed in Ottawa, as an attempt to solve the serious problem of drought and soil drifting across the prairies. In fact, several of the people we interviewed remember the '30s as a time of blinding sand storms which scarred their faces. It was discovered by agricultural scientists that much of the land which was being homesteaded should never have been used for farm land—it was too arid. The solution was to seed this land with grass to be used for grazing, in order to conserve the moisture in the soil. During the three-year survey period, 1935 to 1938, Ste. Madeleine was designated to become part of the community pasture.*

*Under the provisions of the PFRA, people living in these selected areas were entitled to a full federal compensation, providing they had paid all their back taxes on the land. Better quality Crown or municipal land would be offered in exchange for their current land, and families would be assisted in relocating.*

*Unfortunately, in Ste. Madeleine, only one or two families had been able to afford the property taxes for their homesteads over the years. Legally, the majority of the people were therefore squatters on their own land, and were forced to move without any compensation. Their houses were burned, their church was dismantled, and by 1938, the once vital community of Ste. Madeleine had virtually vanished.*

*Today, all that remains of Ste. Madeleine are the stone foundations of the Belliveau School, and the cemetery encircling the mound of grass where the church once stood. The wood from the schoolhouse was salvaged, and through a circuitous route eventually found its way to the Metis home of Yvonne and Fred LeClerc in Victor, Manitoba. The remains of the school now constitute the major portion of their kitchen.*

*The only aspect of the community life which remains today centers around the graveyard which stretches over two acres of land amidst the grazing cattle. The old-timers continue to attend the crumbling graves of their family members. Most of Ste. Madeleine's ex-inhabitants see this as their final resting place.*

*Today, the memories of Ste. Madeleine are still rich and alive among the people who speak in these pages. And the stories of that community—of the family life, the hard work, the simple sharing of friendship, music and dancing are told and retold to children and grandchildren. The history recorded here is a unique one—of a small Metis community in Manitoba that struggled to survive during insufferable times. But this is also a universal story with themes common to all peoples. We hope that our readers, young or old, Metis or non-Metis, will find common threads woven through these stories with which they can all identify.*

V.R.Z.

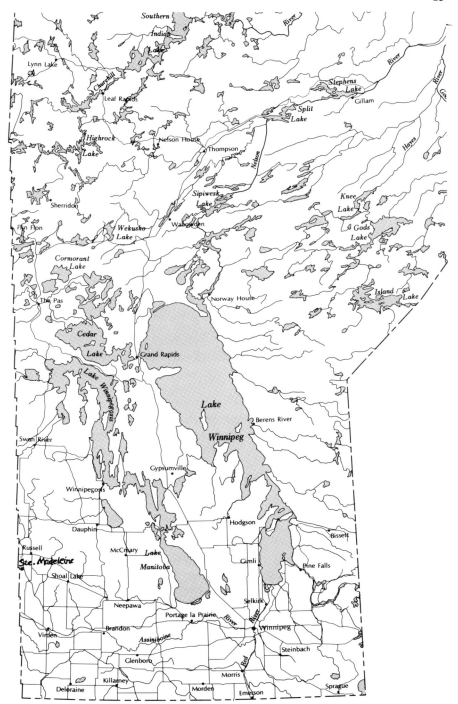

*Ste. Madeleine (1902 - 1940) was located in the southwestern part of the province of Manitoba, on the border of Saskatchewan.*

14

## JOE VENNE

Joe Venne was born November 21, 1906, in Pumpkin Plains, Manitoba, a small district 10 kilometres northwest of St. Lazare. His parents, Alexandre Venne and Elise (nee) Fleury, had four children all together, two boys and two girls. Joe's grandfather, Baptiste Fleury, was one of four Fleury brothers who had come from Baie St. Paul (in the Red River Valley) to homestead in Ste. Madeleine, at the turn of the century.

When Joe was four, his brother, Isadore, was born, and his mother died of complications from childbirth. After this, Joe lived with his grandfather and was also partly raised by his uncle, Pat Bellehumeur, a brother-in-law to Louis Riel.

As a boy of twelve, Joe was obliged to earn a living for his whole family, as his grandfather was too sick to work. He worked for farmers, cutting wood, scrubbing, and tending horses. In the '40s, Joe took up carpentry which became his life's work; he built everything from houses to churches and schools. Joe and his wife, Josephine Vermette, had eight children, six boys and two girls.

Joe now lives in Birtle, Manitoba. He enjoys meeting with his friends and playing bingo almost every night. He is active with the Manitoba Metis Federation [MMF], and attends their meetings regularly.

*Mr. Venne, I want to begin by asking about your past and your background. When and where were you born?*

November 21, 1906. I was born in Pumpkin Plains, Manitoba, about six miles northwest of St. Lazare.

*And does it still exist?*

No. It's in the community pasture now.

*It was made into a pastureland. When was that?*

In 1938.

*This was by the Prairie Farm Rehabilitation Act [PFRA]?*

Right.

*Now, do you remember your mother at all?*

Yes. I remember when my mother passed away.

*What do you remember?*

I was four years old. I remember my dad had me on his knees . . . and he was talking to my mother at the same time. She was telling him what she wanted done for us; to place us in my grandfather's hands. So that's what we did.

*She knew she was dying?*

Yes. And that's the time my brother was born, my young brother. He was born in 1910.

*So your mother died in childbirth?*

After childbirth, yes.

*I see. And what was your brother's name?*

Isadore. Isadore Venne.

*And did he live a long time?*

He passed away in 1954. He's buried across the river, in that graveyard, where you were yesterday. He's buried in there.

*In Ste. Madeleine? Then your earliest memory was of your mother dying. What happened to you then? That was 1910.*

Well, I kept on staying with my grandfather.

*On your father or your mother's side?*

My mother's side.

*What was his name?*

Baptiste Fleury.

*So his name was Fleury. And his wife?*

Cecile Flammand.

*And where did you stay at that time?*

We stayed just in my grandfather's homestead, just north of St. Lazare, about thirteen miles.

*And what kind of man was your grandfather?*

Oh, he was a very good man.

*Did he ever hit you or discipline you?*

No, no. He disciplined me, but in a way that I had to remember not to do it again.

*And your father? What happened to him?*

My father? Well, he went away to North Dakota. He went to visit his brother and he stayed there, for quite a few years. I don't know how long he was in the States. But he came back into Canada down to the St. Ambroise area. And he got married again to a girl by the name of Philomène Ducharme.

*Did they have children?*

No. They had no children.

*So how many children did your mother and father have?*

Four.

*And were you the oldest?*

No, I had a sister older than me, and a sister younger than me.

*Are you the only one still around?*

Yeah. I'm the only one.

*And where did you live with your grandfather?*

We lived on a homestead for quite some time and then we moved to St. Hubert, Saskatchewan. We stayed there a few years. And after that, we moved back into Ste. Madeleine, Manitoba, in 1921.

*Why did you move to Ste. Madeleine?*

Well, my grandfather took sick and he was sick for about two years. He couldn't do anything, he couldn't work. He wanted to be close to his brothers in Ste. Madeleine. And he wanted to be close to his relations. So that's how come we moved there.

*How long had Ste. Madeleine been in existence?*

Oh, as far back as I can remember. I don't know how long; it's been years and years, apparently—one day, when some of his brothers took homesteads there. But his homestead was farther south, about four miles south of Ste. Madeleine in the Red Deer Horn Creek area.

*But no brothers lived in Ste. Madeleine itself?*

Well, the three brothers were living there. His three other brothers.

*Right inside Ste. Madeleine?*

Right in Ste. Madeleine.

*And how much land did they have?*

They had a quarter section each. Which they took in homestead.

*Which is 160 acres. So they were really farmers?*

Well, they were farmers. They had cattle and horses at the time they were in there to start homesteading.

*Did they grow grain?*

Very little. Just enough for feed because at that time there wasn't much land broken and they had to break it with horses, and they didn't break very many acres in a year.

*And how did they make a living?*

Oh, just by working with wood, you know. There was a lot of wood at that time, a lot of good bush and they were selling wood and things like that, and working for themselves at the same time. They used to grow their own gardens. At that time, I suppose, they had the good years because the time we were there we couldn't grow anything.

*Now if I'm right, you were born in 1906, you moved to Ste. Madeleine in 1921. So you were fifteen years old, when you moved there. So you have a pretty good memory of the place. How big was the whole of Ste. Madeleine? How much territory did it cover?*

Well, there were two sections really, one against the other, and down farther there were four more sections up to the Saskatchewan border. That was Ste. Madeleine.

*Was it part of Manitoba? Was it called Ste. Madeleine, Manitoba?*

Yeah, it was called Ste. Madeleine, Manitoba. I don't know where the name came from but when the Metis people settled there, they wanted a church for themselves; they had to go to St. Lazare at the time. And with the horses, it was quite a distance, thirteen, fourteen miles, so they wanted a church and they couldn't get any grant of any kind. At that time there were no grants to be given. So they started holding socials, all kinds of socials, really. The most common was a basket social . . . and they'd sell these baskets and they gathered their money that way to start to build their church. And all the people in the community got together and each of them had to put in so many logs to have enough logs to build the church.

*How many logs?*

Well, I don't know. Approximately each of these families had to bring either 20 or 30 logs. Some brought 30 logs and some brought 20 logs to have enough to build the church. I figure there'd be 60 or 70 logs all together needed to build the frame of the church.

*But if each family brought 20 or 30 logs, then you had more logs than you needed.*

Yeah, well, they didn't all bring them. Some of them supplied work instead of bringing logs. But that was the deal. If one family couldn't bring logs, they did some work, and those, who could, brought logs.

*What year was this?*

Oh, I was about six or seven years old—1912 when they started.

*Where was this?*

In Madeleine. In Ste. Madeleine.

*But you didn't live there until 1921.*

No, but that was the second time we came back.

*So you lived in Ste. Madeleine . . . .*

Before.

*Well, let's go back. Your mother died in 1910, when you were four years old.*

Yeah, she died in Ste. Madeleine.

*So, you were living in Ste. Madeleine when your mother died.*

I was born there, close to Ste. Madeleine but it was called the Pumpkin Plains district.

*How close to Ste. Madeleine?*

It'd be about fifteen or sixteen miles.

*Right. But I'm still not completely clear. You lived in the Ste. Madeleine area?*

Yes. After I was born. See, my mother and them moved into Ste. Madeleine, close to my grandfather's house. They built a house. My father built a house there.

*When your mother died, you moved right into Ste. Madeleine, itself?*

Well, that's where she died.

*At your grandfather's house?*

Yeah.

*She had the baby there. Isadore was born there.*

Was born there, yeah. That's what they called Ellice Municipality.

*And then you lived with your grandfather from 1910 till when?*

Until he passed away in 1933.

*Oh I see. So you lived in Ste. Madeleine from 1910 onwards?*

No, in 1918, we moved into Saskatchewan for a few years.

*For how long?*

We stayed there until 1921.

*Three years. Where did you stay? In a town?*

No, we stayed in a mission in St. Hubert, Saskatchewan. There was a convent and a church. And there were about four priests there. We lived in St. Hubert.

*Okay, let me tell you the story as I understand it, because I'm a little confused. You were born in Pumpkin Plains which was not far from the two sections of land which constituted Ste. Madeleine. And then, when your mother was ready to deliver Isadore, she came from Pumpkin Plains to your grandfather's house.*

No, they had moved there before.

*How soon before?*

Well they moved there . . . I don't remember when they moved there because I was too young . . . .

*Yes.*

But I remember the time my brother was born. My father had come and built a house close to my grandfather's place. And that's where my brother was born.

*Okay. So then, your mother was buried in Ste. Madeleine's Cemetery. Do you know where the grave is?*

Yes.

*Is it marked?*

No, it's not marked. There's bush growing on it now.

*I see. Are you going to put up a marker?*

We're going to put up a stone there for . . . for all the dead people who are in that cemetery.

*You were about two when you moved into Ste. Madeleine?*

Yes.

*Okay, how many families were living in Ste. Madeleine that you remember in 1910, when you first remember that period?*

There were approximately twelve families living there at that time.

*How many people would that be?*

Well, on average, about three to five in each family.

*So would you say 60 or 70?*

Yes, 60 or 70 people living there at that time.

*How was it that they were living there?*

Well, they took homesteads when they were open.

*When was that?*

In the late 1800s and the early 1900s. Because I remember my grandfather talking about homesteads being open up to 1924.

*And to homestead, what were the requirements?*

They had to put ten dollars down and go build on that homestead. They built log houses on the homesteads—and log barns—and moved in there. Then they had to keep improving the homesteads before they could get title deeds.

*Now did your grandfather get a title deed?*

Yes, he did.

*Did you see it?*

No, I don't remember seeing it.

*And once he had title deed, did he have to pay tax?*

Yes. He paid tax.

*To whom?*

To the municipality.

*How much was his tax?*

Oh, I don't remember that. I was too young.

*And did he pay it every year?*

As far as I can remember he did, until we moved into Saskatchewan in 1918.

*And that was because of the flu?*

Yes.

*So he left his land at that time. And he was gone three years. Then he came back in 1921, to Ste. Madeleine.*

Yes.

*To the same homestead?*

No. I bought a place there.

*You did?*

Yes. I was fifteen years old.

*And you lived there alone?*

No. My grandfather moved there with me. And my brother and one of my aunts.

*What did you pay for the homestead? Do you remember?*

I paid $400. It's not a homestead. It's a piece of land that I bought—80 acres. I paid $400 for it.

*Where did you get $400 when you were only fifteen?*

I was working since the time I was twelve years old. That's why I never had a chance to go to school. I worked for farmers.

*And you saved your money.*

Oh yes.

*So when you bought this land, the 80 acres, it was 1921, and you owned 80 acres of land?*

Yes. And I couldn't buy it in my name because I was too young. I had to be 21 to be able to have it registered to my name so I registered it to my grandfather's name.

*Do you have the document?*

No, I haven't.

*Did you ever see it?*

Oh, I saw it but it's lost now.

*And would it be in the municipality of Ellice?*

I suppose so. If it was ever saved, when they destroyed the office of the municipality of Ellice in St. Lazare. That's where all the papers were.

*Did you pay tax on the land?*

Yes, I did.

*How much?*

It wasn't very much. About fifteen, sixteen dollars a year.

*And did you have the money every year to pay it?*

No. When the dry years hit in the 30s, I couldn't make enough money to pay the tax. I just barely made enough for a living.

*So when did you stop paying tax?*

In 1929. That was the last time we paid tax.

*So you continued to live on the land from 1929 until 1939.*

Until 1938. That's when I moved out.

*So for nine years you lived there and you didn't pay anything.*

No, no.

*So who owned the land at that time?*

We were still living there. Nobody ever bothered us until 1938, see.

*And then what happened in 1938?*

Well then, in 1938, we were asked by the municipality to move out as they were going to build a community pasture.

*Who asked you? Who were the men who asked you?*

Mr. Selby. Mr. Selby was the clerk for the municipality of Ellice. Mr. John Selby and Mr. Ben Fouillard.

*And they were fellows paid by the municipality? Or by the PFRA?*

The municipality. They were the council of the municipality.

*And did anyone from the federal government come and talk to you?*

No. We had people come and talk to us, but we didn't know who they were. I remember they came but I couldn't remember their names or whatever.

*So they may have been men from Ottawa?*

Yes, they could have been. But I can't say for sure.

*What did they tell you?*

Well, they told us that they were going to build a pasture and there'd be a lot of cattle in the pasture, and if we moved, that they were going to pay us for our land, and pay us . . . to move. They were going to pay us for moving to wherever we wanted to move. But the people who had land and had paid up their tax, had a chance to choose a piece of land anywhere, on the outside of the community pasture. And that happened, that some took land on the outside.

*Okay, now let me get this straight. Let me tell you how I understand it, and then tell me if I've got it right. You and your family lived from 1929 to 1938, nine years, and you didn't pay tax . . .*

No.

*. . . on these 80 acres of land, because the times were poor, and you didn't have the money.*

Yes.

*So effectively, you lost the land.*

We lost the land, in three years, you see. At that time, if you didn't pay the tax, you lost the land. It was lost but they let us live there.

*But still, no one stopped you from living there.*

No.

*Then in 1935, when the PFRA was put into order, it took three more years for them to come and tell you that it was time for you to move.*

Yes, yes.

*So really, you were squatters on the land.*

Yes, we were.

*Because you didn't pay for it. And even though you were squatters, from a legal point of view, you were offered some money. How much were you offered?*

We were given $150.

*Now who paid you that money?*

The municipality of Ellice.

*Not the government?*

Not the government. If it came from the government, we didn't know anything about it. It must have gone to the municipality, because they didn't give me that all at once. They paid me seventeen dollars a month.

*For how long?*

Until the $150 was paid up.

*And you took the $150?*

Yes, I took it.

*And what happened to your cattle?*

I sold them. And some of them starved. We didn't have feed. We didn't have hay. We had nothing.

*When did these cattle starve?*

That was in the 30s.

*But in 1938, how many cattle did you have?*

I didn't have any. They were all gone then. Whatever little I had, I sold. I sold about four head of cattle, the last bunch in 1936 or 1937. I don't remember the year exactly, but it was in the fall. I shipped the last two cows I had and I never got paid for those cows because they didn't make enough money to pay the freight from Binscarth, Manitoba to Winnipeg. I got a bill from the CPR that I owed them 96 cents for freight on my cows.

*Did you pay it?*

No, I didn't.

*Did they come after you?*

No, nobody came after me.

*What was your family like, because if my calculation is right, in 1938, you were 32 years old?*

Yes, 32.

*So were you married by then?*

Yes, I had my family. I had the kids.

*How many kids?*

There were four kids.

*And what . . . .*

Five!

*Five kids?*

Yeah, there was the baby, yeah.

*And what was your wife's name?*

Josephine.

*And her maiden name?*

Vermette.

*Josephine Vermette. And you had five children?*

Eight.

*You had eight children?*

Six boys and two girls.

*And are they still alive?*

Yes.

*All of them?*

All alive.

*All eight children?*

Yes.

*And what year were you married?*

I never got married. We just lived together from 1931 to 1972.

*Because your wife died then?*

No. She's still living.

*Oh. But you're not living together?*

No. No, we've been separated now since 1972.

*Do you still see her?*

Oh yes. She's in Brandon. I was there visiting with my daughter the other day.

*Oh really. So you just don't live together?*

We just don't live together.

*Why didn't you get married?*

Well, she was married before.

*I see. And did she have children from her previous marriage?*

No. She didn't stay very long with her first husband. She didn't stay very long.

*Right. And, you're Catholic, I take it. Were you pressured by the priests to get married? Did they look down on you?*

One did. One priest in 1938.

*What did he do? What did he say?*

Well, it didn't matter. She couldn't get a divorce because we were Catholic. And we never had any money to pay for a divorce or anything like that, anyways.

*Are you sorry that you're not together still?*

No, I'm not. We didn't get along, so we separated on good terms. She comes and visits once in a while, and I go and visit. If the kids happen to be here, we get together.

*How did you make your living?*

Well, I was a carpenter. I started carpentering after we moved out.

*After you moved out where?*

After we moved out of the pasture.

*Ste. Madeleine. And this was 1938. Where did you go then?*

Just north of Birtle here, about seven miles.

*You had a piece of land?*

No, I moved into a CPR house. CPR had houses built at that time for people coming from the east, to come and start working for farmers here or to start farming. And there was one CPR house that was vacant, so I rented that. And I moved into it and I worked for that farmer for one year.

When I started carpenter work, I moved back into the Binscarth district and I worked around there, until 1957. I built buildings for farmers: houses, barns granaries, whatever. Then in 1957, I moved to Minnedosa and took a job to work for a contractor for three years, building homes, mobile homes. I worked there for three years and I went to a bigger contractor that was building big buildings like schools, churches, hospitals and that. I worked with that contractor for seven years. When I took sick, I quit working for him and after I got better, I went on my own. And I did quite a bit of building after I was on my own, building homes.

*Did you do it all by yourself or did you hire people?*

Well, no. I had my boys helping me. My boys used to work with me. And after my boys were on their own, I hired help. Wherever I worked, I hired somebody.

*Now, let's move back to Ste. Madeleine, because that's really the essence of the story. You began telling me about a church that was being built when you lived in Ste. Madeleine. What year was this church being built?*

In 1913.

*And who was the priest?*

Father Lalonde.

*What language did he speak?*

He'd speak in French and English.

*Fluently?*

Well, yes.

*How old was he then?*

Oh, he was fairly old—he must have been fairly old because he had grey hair. I'd imagine he would be around 48, 49, at that time.

*And was he a good man?*

Oh yes. He was a good priest. He was a good priest, but he was kind of rough on the younger generation, you know.

*What do you mean?*

Well, they used to think he was mean. He was not mean. It's just that he was trying to straighten out people from doing bad things. The people used to think that he'd get mad. But he wasn't mad, he was just preaching loud. That's all.

*And how long did he stay in the community?*

Oh, he didn't stay very long. After that, he passed away. He got too old to conduct the church and also, somebody else took over. I don't remember all the priests.

*You say he passed away. Did he pass away in Ste. Madeleine?*

No. They sent him away to a home someplace. They had special homes for them. So that's where he went.

*So the first priest you really remember is Father Lalonde?*

No, I remember Father DeCorby. He was around at that time but he was a priest who was not stationed in one place. He travelled all over.

*Now he's a famous priest. Tell me about him.*

Well, I don't remember too much about him.

*What did he look like?*

Oh, he was a short fellow, and a heavy-set fellow.

*What language did he speak?*

He spoke French.

*Not English?*

Yes, he spoke English because there were a lot of people around who only spoke English, and were Catholics. So he'd speak in French and then he'd repeat it in English.

*And do you remember anything particular about Father DeCorby?*

No, not too much, because I was too young at the time. All I remember was that he used to go around with a horse and buggy. He'd go around and visit his congregation.

*Anything else special about him?*

Well, any place, any home that he got in—it was his home. He was welcome, and he'd stay there, and he'd eat whatever people would eat—wherever he was. He wasn't a shy man. He was a friend to everyone.

*Was Father Lalonde like that?*

No, he was a little different. He never used to go around to visit the people like Father DeCorby did.

*Now, you say that in 1913, they built this church in Ste. Madeleine. Before that, where did people go to pray?*

To St. Lazare. But it was too far. When they had to use horses, they had to go there the day before and set up a camp and camp there until Monday, then come back on Monday.

*Now, you were about nine when they started to build the church?*

I was seven years old.

*So your memory of the church is sort of a childhood memory. Did you help at all? Do you remember?*

The only way I helped was to peel logs. In the summertime, the bark comes off logs easily. So I used to peel logs. Once they got started, I'd pull the bark off logs.

*As a little child?*

As a little child.

*And then the church was built. And, do you know how big the church was? What were its dimensions?*

Oh the main part was about, I'd say, 28 to 30 feet long. And then the little part at the back was about ten by eight.

*When you say the little part at the back, do you mean the baptismal font? Or the nave?*

No, where there was a platform, built higher—that little back part where the priest had all his equipment and everything in there. That's where he used to stand to preach.

*Did he take confession at the church?*

Yes, there was a confessional there.

*And how many seats were in the church?*

Oh, the church was big enough to seat about 60 to 70 people.

*Do you ever remember it being full?*

Oh yes. Oh, lots of times, we couldn't all get in.

*What about music? Was there any music in the church?*

There was an organ. And there were local people singing hymns.

*We always think of a bell in a church. Was there a bell tower?*

No, there was no bell tower at the time the church was built. But in 1923, 1924, the community started raising money by socials, and things like that, to buy a bell. And we bought a bell and we built a scaffold on the outside of the church close to the door, not too far from the door of the church, and we put the bell up on that scaffold.

*So the church belonged to the people. They built it.*

Yes, they built it.

*They sponsored it. They looked after it?*

Yes.

*And the first priest who was there was Father Lalonde?*

Well, they were both working. When Father Lalonde came, Father DeCorby was here before him.

*But did Father DeCorby see the church first?*

I don't remember if he was ever at the church, but I remember him in St. Lazare.

*Who consecrated the church, do you remember?*

I don't remember that.

*And when the church was built around this time, 1906 to 1913, there were maybe 60 or 70 people living in Ste. Madeleine,—and so the church was built to accommodate that number of people?*

To accommodate that number of people.

*But then you said the church was too small and many people couldn't get in.*

Well, we had the neighboring people, who were Catholic, from St. Joseph and lots of times, from St. Lazare. And there were a few Catholics from Binscarth. We had people coming to church there, when there was a special day, a special church service. And sometimes we got too many people. It was big enough to hold all the people in the community, but when we had the neighboring people, the church got too full.

*Now when you say special people, do you mean Metis people?*

Not special people. A special mass or special occasion of the church.

*But generally, was it only the Metis people who came to the church?*

No, no, no, no. Oh no, there were different kinds of people. Of course they were Catholics, but it was English-speaking people, and Indian-speaking people, the Gambler Reserve was involved and they helped to build that church, too.

*This is a Cree Reserve?*

This is a Cree Indian Reserve, yes.

*Okay now, around 1913, when the church was built, there were only maybe 60 or 70 people in Ste. Madeleine.*

Yes.

*But before we began this interview, you showed me a document. I think it was 1923, and there were 200 people living in Ste. Madeleine.*

Yes.

*So from 1913, when you were seven, until 1918, before the flu and before you left for Saskatchewan for three years, do you remember more people coming into Ste. Madeleine, during that time?*

No, no, they were disappearing instead of moving in. People were moving out.

*Why?*

I can't answer you that . . . maybe on account of the dry air and they couldn't grow anything.

*Even in 1913 and 1914, it was dry?*

Well, it was okay at that time, but since that.

*Sure, but I'm saying that at some point, like 1923, there were 200 people, so it means that from 60 to 70 people in 1913, it grew, within about ten years, by almost three times.*

Well that's true. Well most of them were children, and they didn't all go to church. But when they moved, people moved a way up in the north where there was fishing and trapping. They left this place because it was hard to grow grain or gardens, anything in that area—there was too much sand.

*Well then, I read in one of the documents that when the government set up the PFRA in 1935, the problem was that people started to homestead, at the turn of the century, but there wasn't enough science to know that certain land should never have been used.*

Should have never been used.

*So are you saying that Ste. Madeleine was not really farming land?*

No, it's not. It's not, no.

*It's grazing land?*

Yes, that's it.

*So the government was right in making it into pasture?*

Yes, you're right. It's right. But that's why I say some of the people couldn't understand that. That's why I said that they were pushed out of there. In fact, for myself, I was glad to leave it in one way because there was nothing you could grow there. I put in a crop in 1930, of oats and wheat. I did a little breaking of twelve acres to grow oats, feed for my cattle and horses, and all I got out of that twelve acres was a little bit of feed, about three quarters of a rack full. That's all I got. And all the cattle and horses started starving. And we couldn't sell them. Nobody had money to buy them.

*So, then what's the solution? The government was not discriminating against the Metis people. Nevertheless, a lot of the Metis people feel badly about it. They feel that they've lost their homes and they lost an area they lived in.*

Yes.

*So if you could, how would you solve this problem?*

Well, it's hard to explain, because those people were born and raised there. There was trapping to be gotten, and wood to be gotten and sold. That was their main living for many years. We hauled wood into town to sell because everybody was using wood at the time. I saw up to thirteen or fourteen teams going to Binscarth one day to sell a load of wood each.

*And what did they get paid for a load?*

Well, we got, as little as, a dollar and a half a load in the '30s. But in the days before that, we got about four dollars a cord. If you had a cord of wood, you sold it for four dollars.

*Was that good money?*

That was good money at the time because everything was cheap. You made a good living. And this is how some people made a living, and were able to hang on to their land. Just by selling wood in the winter. And it was the people who had horses and cattle, at the beginning, before the hard times, who were able to hang on.

*So if we could both go back to Ste. Madeleine, like in the old days, we wouldn't see very many farms, because things didn't grow.*

No. No.

*We would see cattle.*

Yes. You'd see cattle, because they used to take a permit in to where the hay grew, and the fellows that didn't have the money couldn't pay for the permit. So this is where a lot of conflict came from because the poor people couldn't get a permit there. They didn't have the dollar to pay for the hay permit.

*Where would they get the hay from?*

Well, there were some low places where you could get the hay. There was a low place there that we used to cut. Maybe four or five families would get 20 or 30 tons out of it when it was growing.

*Okay, we know that 200 people, including children, lived there at one time. Were there ever anymore living there?*

Oh yes. There was.

*How many? Can you give me a number?*

Well, I'd imagine there'd be another 50 or 60 people.

*Okay, then 260 is the most that ever lived in Ste. Madeleine?*

As far as I know, yes. Some sections were homesteaded and others just had people living on them.

*Squatting?*

Yes.

*And there were some people who had cattle, like you did. And you had a house or two houses?*

One house. There was already a house on the property.

*Right. And you paid the tax for it until 1929.*

Yes.

*So you lived there. And did you clear land every year?*

No, not every year but I cleared it one year, the last time in 1929, that's when I cleared land.

*And you paid your tax that year?*

Yes, I paid my tax that year.

*And after that you just couldn't do that?*

No, I couldn't pay tax.

*And from 1921 until 1929, how did you earn your living?*

Well, by working. By working for farmers. I used to go and take a job for the summer, six or seven months at a time. And then I'd take time in the fall to put up a few loads of hay, where there was hay, the little bit of hay that we got. I took time to go and put it up and keep it for feed for the winter.

*Okay now, you were a bachelor at that time. You didn't live with anyone, and you were still very young . . . .*

No, I lived with my grandfather and my aunt and my brother.

*In this house?*

In this house. I had to earn a living for them.

*Okay, and then your father had gone south and you really hadn't seen him since you were about four years old. So how long was it before you saw your father?*

I saw him again in . . . oh, it was about 1928, when he came back.

*So you hadn't seen your father for about 20 years. Were you angry with him because he had gone away?*

No. No, not at all.

*And when you saw him for the first time, tell me, can you remember how you felt that minute?*

Oh, I hugged him . . . I was glad to see him.

*And was he glad to see you?*

Oh yes. Then he stayed with us for about a year after he come back.

*And what kind of a man was your father?*

Oh, he was a real good man. A good worker. He was a good man, friendly with everybody.

*And did he treat you specially?*

Oh yes. He treated us good. After he come back. But when he went away, we never heard from him. Only maybe once, that I remember. The time he got married, with his second wife.

*And how did he show his love for you. How, when you . . . .*

He used to work and help me, after that.

*Was he affectionate? Did he ever kiss you, or . . . .*

Well, no, because we were men. You know, man to man.

*So he didn't go in for that.*

But we used to hug each other. Just . . . lots of times.

*Did he give you presents?*

Oh yes, oh yes.

*Like what?*

Oh, all kinds of things; harnesses he brought me one time. And things like that, anything that was usable, in the family.

*And he lived in the same house with you, then?*

For a while, about one year, in 1928.

*Now, when your grandfather lived with you—this was your mother's father,—and when your father lived with you, did they contribute to the food, did they buy food, did they give money to the house?*

Oh yes, oh yes. He used to go to work. He'd go to work, and he'd come back on the weekend . . . .

*With groceries?*

. . . and bring groceries and money for the house and keep the house going.

*Who did he give the money to?*

He used to give it to me or to my grandfather. My grandfather was the main one. If I went and worked and I came back home, and I had money left to keep, I'd give it to him and he'd keep the money.

*He'd save it?*

Oh yes.

*Did you put it in the bank?*

No, we never had money in the bank at that time.

*Just in a tin pot or something.*

Yep, yep.

*Now we've spent a lot of time talking about land and people, and all the rest of that. But there was another side of the life that we haven't touched on—the Metis life. At what point did you realize that you were a Metis? Did the word Metis mean anything to you?*

As far back as I can remember, we were called Metis. It doesn't really mean anything better or worse than another nationality. It means we have a certain amount of Indian blood in us. We are mixed people. I first met French people, that were called Metis, in St. Hubert, Saskatchewan.

*But this was 1918 to 1921.*

Yes. And when they came to us, when they came to our home, they said, "Oh, you are Metis."

That's the only time I heard about Metis people, which we used to call "michif". It didn't mean anything to us. No. Because it's not right—the right word is Metis but that came from the east.

*You say that Metis means that you have Indian blood.*

Yes, you're half and half, with Indian blood. You could be Scotch or English or French. There could be anything—Ukrainian, whatever, you name it—but you're half and half.

*Do you know of any Indian ancestors? Do you know if there were some Indian people in your family?*

No, I don't know that. But my grandparents were Metis. They had a little bit of Indian blood in them because they were married to people who had Indian blood in them— Indian people.

*Do you know which tribe?*

No. I don't.

*Do you speak any Indian languages?*

Very little. I understand a little bit of it, the Saulteaux Indian and the Cree Indian.

*So you understand Saulteaux and Cree. And did your grandfather ever talk about his Indian grandmother or . . . .*

Oh, yes.

*And did he ever tell you her name?*

Yes.

*What was her name?*

Oh boy, now you've got me . . . oh, sometimes I remember that name, but I can't get it.

*And yet, if you see other Metis people, what do you have in common with them? You speak English.*

I speak English. I speak a little bit of Cree, a little bit of Saulteaux, I speak French, but my best language is French really.

*That's your mother tongue?*

My mother, yes. My mother and father. They both spoke French.

*So did you ever experience any discrimination? Did people ever call you names when you were younger?*

Oh, yes. Lots.

*Like what?*

Lots. Oh, they'd call you—they'd give you all kinds of names, Indian names. They'd figure you were almost a purebred Indian. But you were not, you were mixed, and that's what they didn't like. They accepted and respected the pureblood Indians, at one time. But when the mixed come, they figured that the mixed people were bad people, worse than others. This is what made a lot of conflict, between the white people and the Indian people and the Metis people.

*Tell me how you were discriminated against, when you think back.*

Well, they would call us different kinds of names.

*Who?*

The white people. The English and Scotch people.

*Give me the names of those people.*

Well, I can't give you the names of those people now. There were too many. I don't know their names. Lots of them, you didn't know a person, and if he saw that you had a little bit of Indian blood, they'd come to insult you if they wanted to insult you. And that's where a lot of fights started from. A lot of trouble.

*Did you ever get into a fight?*

No, not really. Because I used to tell them it didn't matter what kind of blood you got in them, you're still a Canadian. This is what I always thought. A Canadian is a Canadian. That's all that matters, not what nationality he had in him. I never got into trouble for a thing like that. I tried to explain to them, but lots of them didn't . . .

specially after the beer parlor was open, there was a lot of trouble about it, you know, a lot of trouble. A lot of trouble.

*You mentioned the beer parlor. Was drinking a large part of the life?*

Yes.

*Was alcoholism a big problem?*

A big problem.

*In Ste. Madeleine?*

All over. As far as that goes, Ste. Madeleine just the same.

*Way back in 1920?*

When the parlors opened. No, they didn't open here until 1928.

*And before that ? Was there any alcoholism?*

Very little. The only alcohol you got you had to wait for a long time, a week or so before you got it, cause you had to go for a permit, you had to send for liquor. But before that, apparently, there were bars that were open, that would serve liquor in there. But there'd been a lot of trouble in Binscarth here. My grandfather used to tell me there used to be a lot of trouble in the bar. It used to be because there were lots of nationalities. But now it's different. They accept us now. Because we mix with them, you know.

*We were talking about what a Metis is, and you said that there is no difference. Can you tell me if there was any special Metis culture? I know you were a chairman and a vice-chairman of the MMF and so you mixed with people who had similar backgrounds. Culturally, was there a special music? Were there special stories or history that only the Metis people have that other Canadians, Ukrainian-Canadians, or German or Jewish, or French-Canadians don't have?*

Well, in some style, yes. There is because we had parties in different ways. We were a nation of people that liked pleasure, you know, and had a lot of parties. If they had any sense, they'd have a party every night. But a lot of the other people didn't do that; if they had a party a month, they were happy. But the Metis people, they were a people that liked pleasure, you know, and there was a lot of partying. Every week. We never missed—twice a week, three times a week. When it came to the holidays, Christmas and New Year's, we used to go for two, three weeks at a time, dancing every night, partying every night. Other people didn't have that style. This is where the difference is.

*You say partying, dancing. What kind of dances?*

All kinds of square dancing.

*Jigs?*

Jigs, square dances, and the waltz. But the most important part was the square dancing. They'd square dance most of the time, and then, once in a while, just for the people to take a break, they'd play a jig, so we had the jig dancer on the floor.

*To dance, you need music. What kind of music did you have?*

Fiddle. Mostly fiddle.

*One, two? Three?*

Sometimes there were two. We were lucky when we could get two because it was better music.

*Who was the fiddler? When you grew up?*

Well, there were quite a few fiddlers. My uncles, themselves, were playing fiddle.

*What were their names?*

William and John Fleury. And Joe Bellehumeur, my uncle or my auntie's husband, you know.

*And they were the fiddle players?*

They were the fiddle players. There used to be a lot of fiddle players. One of my grandfather's relatives, by the name of Flammand, used to play the fiddle a lot. Oh, there used to be a lot of fiddle players. You could go anywhere. One of the Bouchers from the community and his son were fiddle players. We were never short of fiddlers.

*What songs did they play? Do you remember the names of the songs? Special names?*

Oh no, I don't remember. They were reels, really, not songs. And in 1928, 1929, my brother was the best violin player around.

*Isadore?*

Isadore Venne. That's him there. Sitting up there.

*There's a photo of him here. Did he live with you in Ste. Madeleine?*

Yes.

*He did. Did he marry?*

No, he was never married. He passed away in 1955. He was buried on his birthday.

*And how old was he when he died?*

He was about 45.

*And he was a bachelor. He's a handsome man. And he was never interested in getting married? How come?*

He was a sick person. He'd been sick since he was about five years old. He lived with me. This is why I'm telling you that I had to work to earn a living for them because my grandfather was home to look after him and my aunt. And I had to work to buy, to bring in the grub. You didn't get welfare at that time.

*What was your grandfather's name again?*

Baptiste Fleury.

*And his wife died in the flu of 1918. And he never got married again?*

No. He took sick in 1920 and we had to send him to Regina, and I had to pay the train to take him to Regina. There was no ambulance at that time. They took him by train. And they sent him back, and they said they couldn't cure him. There was no cure for him, so he came home. He was never able to work after that. So I had to work.

*What was wrong with him?*

I don't know. I don't know. Something was wrong in his . . . inside.

*But still he lived a long time.*

He lived up till 1933.

*What about your grandfather on your father's side?*

Oh I saw him when my mother died. I saw him at that time. I never saw him again.

*That was in 1910. Where did he go?*

To the States. They lived in the States. In Dakota.

*He came for your mother's funeral?*

Yes. And they stayed there awhile, for the rest of that winter.

*What do you remember of him, when you were four?*

I remember him with a long white beard, and he was a big man, a fairly big man, with big bones, you know. He wasn't what you'd call a fat man. He was tall. He was a nice man to me, to us anyway. My grandmother was the same—nice. They looked after us for a little while after my mother passed away. They stayed with my grandfather and my father.

*Okay, we dealt a little with the music, the fiddle playing, and the partying. Was alcohol something that made its way into these parties? Do you remember, was there a lot of booze?*

Not too much. No, because people had to send for booze and had to wait a long time for it to come, and also sometimes it didn't come, at that time. But in the later years, they started making their own.

*When? What years?*

Oh, I'd say in about 1926. They started making their own brew, but there never was too much of it. You know, it's not everybody that made it. It's just some that made it.

*And it's not everyone that drank it?*

Not everyone drank it. When these beer parlors opened in 1928, or something, and they brought the beer in, then there was a lot of trouble. Since that, there's been a lot of trouble.

*Okay now, if we could go back to Ste. Madeleine during the period you were there, the '20s and '30s, how big would those log houses be?*

Oh, some of them were small. Our house was about 20 by 24 feet, with two small bedrooms. And then the kitchen joined into them.

*And how was it heated.*

Wood. We had a kitchen stove and a bunk stove, we called it. The houses were warm because they had maybe only two little windows.

*Glass windows?*

Yes, glass windows.

*With a sealing to it? Were they sealed against the cold?*

No, no. We didn't worry about that in those days.

*Did these houses ever burn down? Were there ever any fires?*

No, not too often. Very rare. There were one or two. One time, they had left fire in the stove and they went away, see. And a spark flew out because the front of the stove was open. Started a fire, I suppose.

*Did you have a fire department?*

Oh no. No, people used to run over there and help the neighbour put out a fire with water and bags and pails. You'd get a pail of water, soak your bag in there and fight the fire, throw water on the fire. That was the only way. We never had a fire brigade of any kind.

*How did the community clear the garbage away?*

Oh, they just threw it out there in the bush and burned it.

*And what about toilets? Were there septic tanks?*

No, there were no septic tanks. They were all outside toilets. And lots of times, people didn't have toilets. They'd just go and use the barn.

*What about water? Where did you get your water from?*

We had wells. And then creeks. Springs. You know, there's some springs, water comes out. Lots of people have spring water, and lots, like us, had wells. We had a well at home.

*Did you have stores right inside Ste. Madeleine?*

Oh, yes. Yes.

*How many stores?*

Just one.

*And who owned it?*

First of all, the first store that was there, my grandmother's brother had the store. Roger Flammand. He had a store in the post office. And then after that, we had a school teacher that came and had a store in Ste. Madeleine. And he was teaching school.

*What was his name?*

Poirier from Montreal.

*That was the second storekeeper?*

Yes, well, there was a Ducharme that had a little grocery store. Just groceries, you know, nothing else. Just like sugar, tea, lard, things like that. And baking powder, flour, and stuff like that.

*You said a post office. There was a post office there?*

There was a post office there. We had a post office the same place where he had a little store.

*How much did it cost to mail a letter? In those days?*

Three cents.

*And did you get mail very often?*

Once a week.

*What did you get?*

Well, we got the *Winnipeg Free Press*, and sometimes, a letter or two. And the *Country Guide*. We used to send for the *Country Guide*. A dollar for three years, I think it was.

*What was that?*

It's a paper, a farmer's paper, really. There were a lot of things in there about farming. It came once a month. I got some right here in my place. That was 1918-19. Right there.

*You still have original copies?*

I got them.

*And the post office got mail once a week, a delivery once a week?*

Yes, the mailman used to get his team of horses and go and pick up the mail in Binscarth, and brought it to the post office in Ste. Madeleine, usually on a Friday. And when that Flammand moved away to Camperville, he quit the post office. And Joe Boucher took the post office over at the end of the '20s, the beginning of the '30s.

*And he was the storekeeper then.*

He was the storekeeper. He just passed away in 1985. His wife, Agnes, is still living.

*And were they sort of rich people, the Bouchers?*

They were not rich, but they were making a good living. They could make a living. They had cattle, you know. They had kept cattle that they could make a living from. They had the post office, too. Other people didn't have the cattle, didn't have the horses. They just went out to work for other people to bring home the groceries.

*Now, did you have any other kind of entertainment like radios?*

Nope. We had a gramophone.

*Do you still have one?*

Yes.

*The original one?*

No, no. I bought this one later in an auction sale. The other one, I sold not too long ago. And it must have been about 1942 when I sold the old one with the round record on it, like a tube record.

*Now, if we could go back again, did you have any police in the village?*

No, no. The police had to come from Russell, Manitoba.

*Mounties?*

Yes, the Mounties.

*And did they ever come to the community?*

Oh, yes. Some people were making this, whatever they call the homebrew. And a lot of times, they used to come out there to try and catch these people.

*Did they ever catch them?*

Some of them. Not too often.

*Did people look out for each other?*

They looked out for each other.

*So if they saw the Mounties, they would tell their neighbour?*

Yes. If the first neighbor saw them, the word was at the other end. They could get to them before the Mounties got there. [Laughs]

*So the people really took care of each other.*

Yes, they did. They did. We used to help each other a lot.

*Were there ever any fights?*

Oh, sometimes there was a little fight, but never anything bad.

*Give me an example of an incident when there was bad blood between people.*

Well, as far as I know, that never really came until way later, in the beginning of the '40s.

*Well, but Ste. Madeleine wasn't there in the '40s.*

No, no. I don't mean Ste. Madeleine. I mean among Metis people.

*No, I'm talking about Ste. Madeleine.*

Oh, no. Over there, there was very rarely a bad fight. There was fight but it wasn't fighting that one got hurt bad.

*Were there ever any fights over girlfriends? Or . . . .*

Not too often. No, not too often. I think I just heard of one time when a fight was about that, but not that many.

*Tell me the story.*

Well, it was just the same girl going with two different guys, and one got jealous of the other. They started scrapping at the dance, and in no time, they were settled. So that was the end of it.

*And who did she eventually settle with?*

Oh, she settled with her first boyfriend. [Laughs]

*And what were their names?*

Oh, I'm awful for getting names. And I know them so well. Sometimes, I'd be sitting there and I can't get the name, but it was Ducharme. I was trying to remember his first name. That's the only one that I know that had a fight on account of a girl. But he's dead now. He's passed away. His name was Ducharme. And he had that trouble with a Desjarlais.

*And the girl?*

And the girl was a Vermette.

*Was there childbirth out of wedlock?*

Yes, but that didn't come about until in the '30s, in the hard times. Some made a mistake and couldn't marry the girl cause there was no money to be able to . . . .

*But before that? What about in the '20s and before that?*

No, there was not too much then.

*Was there a lot of "easy sex"?*

Not too much. At that time, girls were kept at home and the parents were pretty strict about the girls. If you wanted to go see a girl, you had to see her in the house. You couldn't take her out to a dance, too often. That didn't come until late in the '30s.

*Okay, now we're dealing with the community of Ste. Madeleine and what it was like. You say that people helped each other.*

Yes. If anyone happened to be sick or if anything happened that he was stuck, the people would go and do some work and give them the money. Free work. If they had to go to town with a load of wood and sell it to bring them groceries, they did it.

*Can you give me any specific examples? Do you remember it ever happening for a friend of yours or for yourself?*

Yes, yes. When people were sick, they couldn't work. They couldn't earn their living, or anything. They couldn't go and get anything. Like when my grandfather was sick, I was stuck because I was trying to work but I had to be home to look after him. Well, I got pretty hard up. My cousins, the Bellehumeurs and the Fleurys, got together and went out and cut some poles and sold them. They helped me out for groceries and stuff that I needed. We did that for each other. When I was well enough, I helped a lot of people. Say somebody died, and they needed help to dig the graves, or they needed help in getting food, I'd go to town and bring them stuff to help them and I'd go and do a lot of work for them. And everybody did that. The Pelletiers, his dad, his uncle, if we needed help, if we needed somebody to come and help us, they didn't charge us for the help. They'd come and help us get ahead.

*Did you sometimes have to ask?*

No. Never. If a person was sick, we used to go and see him. "Oh, we'd better go and see. Maybe they need something," that's the way people thought, at that time. We weren't asked to go. Before we were asked, we'd go.

*It's not like that today. Are you sad to see that change?*

Very sad. That was a good way. Everybody should do it the same way. I know one person whose barn burned down and he didn't have a barn for the winter, and his horses and cattle were outside. He had a few cattle and a couple of milk cows. And we all went. There were about thirteen of us that went. And we built him a stable in one day.

*This was in Ste. Madeleine?*

Yeah, in Ste. Madeleine.

*What year?*

Oh, in the early '30s, but we did that every year. We did that all the time. We helped each other.

*Do the Metis people still have that spirit?*

No. No, not now. If you need help, no. You got to pay for it.

*Now, you spoke about your grandfather having to go for treatment in Saskatchewan, and about the fact that today, there's welfare, there's government medical service, and so on. Which was better? The old days or the present day?*

Well, I don't know. I think in the present day, you get it for nothing. You don't have to pay for it. But at that time, you had to pay. But then in the old days, people seemed to be more friendly than they are today. Today, there's a lot of people that won't go and help you if you need help. You've got to pay for that help. But at that time, you didn't have to. I'd sooner live in the old style than I do now. In the old days, there seemed to be more pleasure because you got along with all people. And you weren't scared of getting stuck and being home with sickness without any help.

*I'd like to tell you a little story. Yesterday, George Pelletier, George Ducharme and I were at the Ste. Madeleine graveyard, and George suddenly said, "You know, I had a dream last night. I dreamt that I was back in Ste. Madeleine, and all the old people were there talking to me and they were happy. I got up and I was so lonesome I couldn't go back to sleep again. And you came. There were five of us, four of us, and you took me to Ste. Madeleine, to this place. It must have been a vision."*
*If we could go back to Ste. Madeleine, do you think we could find happiness? Were the people there happier than they are today?*

Oh, yes. Oh, yes. That's why I say, everybody was friendly and happy. We knew that if we got stuck, we knew some of the help would come. Not like today.

*Do you ever dream about these things?*

Yes, yes. Oh, lots of times. Because there, it was really a pleasure to be alive.

*Even though you worked very hard?*

Oh, yes. Work didn't mean anything to us at that time. Because we were young. We were all happy, with no worries.

*If you close your eyes for a minute, and you think back about Ste. Madeleine, whose faces and whose voices do you hear?*

All my friends. All the people who were my friends. All the people around us. And they were all friendly. Even the school teacher. We were happy, really happy. And there were no troubles of any kind. No serious trouble.

*Who was the school teacher toward the end?*

Mr. Blouin.

*What kind of a man was he?*

Oh, he was a good man.

*What language did he speak?*

French and English.

*What language did he teach?*

French and English. But there were not many that took French because they were used to English teachers.

*What grades were taught at the school?*

Oh, anywhere from grade one to seven or eight. We had a teacher that taught up to grade nine, at one time.

*Did you have any people there that went on to high school?*

No, at that time it was hard. There's a fellow who's living here now, who should have gone on to high school. But at that time, it's not like today, there wasn't enough room in the school to send them all into high school. So they had to go by vote. Which one will go to school? So this fellow lost by one vote. So the other girl went. There was a girl. They went through some tests, you see. Some arguments came up that he was supposed to go. He should have gone because he answered the questions sooner than the girl did.

*And the man's name?*

Paul Fleury. He's still here.

*How old is he?*

He's two years younger than I am. He's 77.

*He's somebody we should talk to then?*

He's good if you can find him. He's a hard man to find. [Laughs]

*What was the name of the school?*

Belliveau School.

*You said you went to school for six months. Who was your teacher?*

Well, I had a different kind of teacher. There was a sister in St. Hubert, Saskatchewan. I went to school there for three months.

*This was between 1918 and 1921?*

Yes. And then we moved into Manitoba. I went to school for another three months.

*Why didn't you continue?*

I had to go out to work. I only had a chance of maybe two or three months after the harvest was finished, to go for a little while. And then I had to work to earn a living.

*Are you sorry that you never went to school?*

I am. I am. I wish I had a chance to go to school. But I couldn't. I had to go and work. I had to go and earn a living, from the time I was twelve years old. And I only had a chance to go to school for six months in my life.

*Did most of the people there have only a little schooling?*

Yes, because most of them had to go to work. People who had children, lots of them, had to make them quit school to go out and do some work to earn a living. Sometimes it would take two, three weeks at a time before they would come back. And the kids would go to school for just a few days. Then they would have to leave to work again. At that time, the law was not as strict as it is today, for the schooling of the children. They could go away any time, and it didn't matter when they left or when they came back. And when they came back, they could go back to school and start where they had left off.

*Now, you spoke before about the culture, the music. As it's getting close to lunchtime, and our stomachs are beginning to rumble, when you think back to Ste. Madeleine, can you talk about the culinary culture, the culture of food. What kind of food was prepared? In fact, did your grandfather make the food? Was he the cook?*

Yes. Most of the time after he took sick, he cooked. But when he was able to work, we had to do the cooking ourselves.

*So if I could go back to your home, in Ste. Madeleine, what kind of food would you be feeding me?*

Well, the only food we had was potatoes and meat. We never had pies or cakes or pastry of any kind, unless my aunties or my oldest sister would come and visit us and cook for us. But otherwise, we were always cooking the same thing, potatoes and meat, if we had the meat. But sometimes we didn't have the meat. We'd have soup. Potato soup or whatever we could make.

*What kind of meat?*

Usually wild meat. Rabbits, chickens, ducks, whatever we could get. In the fall, after the deer season opened, we never worried whether it was open or not, if we wanted a jumper, then we'd go out and shoot him. The most meat that we ever had was rabbit and partridge and chickens and ducks.

*You say a jumper. What's a jumper?*

A deer. A mule deer. There were lots of them around.

*And what about vegetables?*

Well, that's what I mean. Vegetables, if you had a good year to be able to grow a few, you had vegetables, but it's not every time you could grow some because the land over there was all sandy. And if you didn't look after your garden, and water it every day, you didn't grow any vegetables.

*What kind of vegetables did you have?*

The only kind of vegetables you can grow fairly easy was onions and radishes and stuff like that. Carrots.

*Cabbage?*

It was hard to grow cabbage. I never saw any good cabbage in the sandy land.

*Lettuce?*

Lettuce. Lettuce would grow easily.

*And tomatoes?*

No, we never had tomatoes in our garden.

*What about fruit?*

We used to have lots of wild fruit. We had saskatoons, cranberries, raspberries, and strawberries that grew anyplace on the plains. You could see thousands of people picking the wild ones.

*And did you make jam out of them?*

Oh, yes. Yes, preserved jam. We used to have cord sealers, and we canned them, and put them down in the basement. Well, there was no basement in most of the houses. There was just a cellar.

*In Ste. Madeleine?*

Yes.

*Okay. Food is very close to health. If people got sick, how were they taken care of?*

Well, we had to try and get what they wanted to eat.

*I'm talking about doctors.*

Oh, doctors. Well, doctors never worried about food at that time.

*Did they have doctors to visit sick people?*

Well, when we went and got them, yes.

*What did they charge?*

Oh, it just depends . . . sometimes they'd charge maybe four, five dollars, maybe two or three dollars. Just enough for their travel, as it was hard times, you know. Lots of times, the drugs were only a dollar and a quarter, a dollar, or fifty cents, whatever the case may be. And it was hard to pay for. But sometimes we managed to be able to pay the doctor's transportation. And lots of times, we had to go and meet him somewhere.

*So, who were the doctors who came to Ste. Madeleine?*

Dr. Gilbart. Dr. Gilbart from Spy Hill, Saskatchewan.

*Gilbart. And who else?*

Dr. Torrance. Oh, there was another doctor before that. I might remember the name later. But Dr. Gilbart was about the best doctor we had. He's the one that looked after our community more than any other doctor. It didn't matter what kind of weather. I saw that doctor come in, about twelve, thirteen miles distance from Spy Hill, coming in to you on snowshoes, just to come and see a patient. And he never charged. If we had money, if we could pay him, we did give him some money, but if we couldn't pay him, it didn't matter to him. He'd come anyway.

*What years were these?*

Oh, that was in the 20s and 30s, until he passed away in the late 30s.

*You remember when he died?*

Oh yes. He was pretty old, too, when he was doing that. He'd be a man around 55, 60.

*Was there folk medicine?*

Yes.

*Who practised it?*

Oh, they all did. Some of them didn't know as much as others. There was Mrs. Joe Bercier; she was a midwife. She born a lot of children around here. And there was a Mrs. Boucher, Lena Fleury's mother, doing the same thing. They were like doctors.

*Now, what about welfare because there was a four year old girl you looked after in 1933? Can you tell me that story?*

Yes, my aunt took sick and had to go to the hospital. So there was no place that she could leave her little girl but with me because she was born in our home and she didn't know where else to leave her little girl. So I took her in, but I was having a hard time making a living because I had kids, too, at that time. So this is why I tried to get help of the municipality to support that girl.

*And they helped her?*

Yes. They didn't help her with cash, but I had to go to a store and take five dollars worth of groceries.

*Which town?*

Binscarth, or St. Lazare, either town. Was the same. Didn't matter where we went.

*Did other people in Ste. Madeleine get help like this, as well?*

Same thing.

*So there was a kind of support system?*

Yes. They used to call it relief.

*Now, you say your aunt got sick and had to go to the hospital. Where was the hospital?*

In Russell, Manitoba.

*And did she have to pay to go to the hospital?*

No, we took her out there.

*But did she have to pay for the bed?*

No. There was a . . . I don't know who paid for the bed. We never had to pay for the bed because that came through the municipality.

*And what about the doctors in the hospital?*

Same thing.

*What was wrong with her?*

Oh, she had stomach trouble.

*And they fixed her up?*

Well, they did. They did, but in the years to come she had the same trouble, you know.

*How long did she stay in the hospital that time?*

Oh, she stayed there about eight or ten days.

*And how many children did she have? Just this one girl?*

Just this one.

*This one girl. Who is still alive?*

Yes.

*What's her name?*

Lena. She was a Fleury, but she married a Drielick.

*It's not the Lena Fleury we're going to see?*

Yes. No, no, no. She's a different one. That little girl I'm talking about, she got married to George's Pelletier's father. She was Mrs. Harry Pelletier.

*And then what happened? They separated?*

They separated. Oh, a long time ago, during the war. When the war started, Harry joined the army. He went away and he met another woman out there, I guess, and never came back.

*Did you ever think of joining the Canadian army in the Second World War?*

Yes. That's where I found out I had TB. That was 1939.

*So you never saw any service.*

No. I went to see the doctor and when I saw the doctor, he says, "It's not clear. Something's not clear." He said there was a travelling clinic in St. Lazare the next week on a certain day. He said, "I'd like you to go to that clinic."

So I says, "Okay. I can't work. I feel weak." I was having a bad cold and coughing all the time, you know. So I went to that clinic. I hired Mr. Boucher who I was talking about, who passed away. I hired him to take me there, and I went to that clinic, and they told me I had tuberculosis and I had to go to a sanitorium.

*And you went? Where?*

In St. Vital or St. Boniface. I was there for two years.

*And then? What did they tell you when you left?*

They told me that I would only have about 90 days to live.

*How did you react then? Did you cry? Did you get upset?*

No, it didn't worry me. I came home.

*And when you came back, you came back to where?*

I came back to Binscarth, here. My family had rented a house about halfway between Binscarth and the Assiniboine Valley, west along the Assiniboine River.

*This was your wife and your eight children?*

Yes, and the children.

*So, who supported them during this time?*

The municipality.

*I see. They were on welfare?*

No, it's not welfare. At that time, it was relief. There was no welfare. And they were getting very little. Just enough for the food.

*So you came back, and you got well again.*

Yes, I got well.

*Who helped you to get well?*

An old fellow, by the name of Paul Ducharme. He's dead now. He died just the fall after.

*From Ste. Madeleine?*

He used to be in Ste. Madeleine but he lived at the time, in Selby Town. That's where he was.

*You met him in Winnipeg?*

No, no. I met him here. I knew him before, pretty well all my life. So he was here. He used to like me a lot, so he came to visit me one time. And he asked me what was the trouble so I told him. He says, "Would you try a drug? If I give you one?"
I says, "I'd try anything." Because I was lying in bed, couldn't do anything. I couldn't work. I was having a hard time to move around.
So he says, "I'll bring you some stuff." And he came back about two days later, with two gallons. Glass jugs, he had two of them full.

*What color were they?*

Just a kind of brownish color.

*What did it taste like?*

Not too bad. Just taste like a weed of some kind. I didn't find it too much different than the tea.

*Did you heat it? Did you warm it up?*

No, no. I just kept it cool.

*And how much did you drink?*

All I could drink, everyday. Then I got better. I was getting better all the time, and towards the fall, when he came one time, he brought three gallons. And I used to give him a package of tobacco or a pound of tea or something like that. And he was very happy.
And he said, "Well, I'm going to show you what I'm giving you for medicine. When you're okay, when you can come down, I'll take you in the bushes, and I'll show you what you're drinking."
And when I was feeling better, I started working. I was feeling so well, I started stooking and thrashing and cutting wood.

*For the farmers?*

For the farmers. Yes, I got better. That last bunch that he brought, the three gallons? I was out working down east of Binscarth and when I came home, they told me that he was sick. I started that night for the lake. Sunday morning, he was dead. So, I never had the chance to speak to him. But I kept on drinking that stuff. I finished it off, you know, all that he gave me. He used to take the empty jugs down and fill them up. And bring them back.

*What year was this?*

In 1942 to 1943. One year. And I've been up since that. And I was given only 90 days to live when I came out. Because they couldn't do anything with me. I wanted to have an operation when they told me I might have to go for one. But they didn't give it to me. They said it wouldn't do any good, anyway.

*Did you ever go back to see your doctors?*

Oh yes. I built a house across the river from the sanitorium in St. Boniface. So I went to see my doctors, and they were sure surprised. And I'll tell you this: they're both dead now, and I'm still living.

*Mr. Venne, the story of Ste. Madeleine was told to me this way: it had been a Metis community since the turn of the century; the Metis got land there because they were promised land by the 1870 Manitoba Act; and in 1938, the Metis were pushed out by the PFRA. Their homes were burned; their church was made into a pigsty; and the people had to move to different areas. Can you tell me what actually happened? When did the Metis people first find out they were going to be taken off that land?*

They started in the fall of 1937, which is the first time that I heard they were planning to use the land for pasturing.

*What did they tell you?*

Well, they told me that they were going to use that land for pasturing cattle. They were going to fence it and keep cattle there. And they said when the people who lived there moved, they would get help for so much, and the ones that owned land would get land back on the outside of the pasture, anywhere they could find land that was equivalent to the land they had in Ste. Madeleine. And some of them didn't own land, didn't own anything, you might as well say. They were supposed to be given enough money to move. So this is what a lot of people did. And they were paid transportation. The moving was paid through the municipality, and I guess the money came from the community pasture.

*The federal government?*

The federal government, likely. I never really studied it at that time.

*Now, you say that "they told me". Who were they?*

The municipality of St. Lazare, John Selby, Ben Fouillard, and there was, I forget his first name, but his last name was Little. They were the people who we talked to. Mr. John Selby was the secretary. Ben Fouillard was on the council, and Ed Seymour.

*When they told you this, were they mean and nasty people?*

No, no. Oh, no, no, no. They weren't.

*Did they know what it meant to the Metis people?*

Yes, they did. They did.

*And were they sympathetic to what was happening?*

No, they didn't say that either. But they weren't mean. They came and talked to you nicely, if you wanted to go. But then, when they talked to some of the people who didn't like to move out of there, you know, then they said they were going to force them out. They didn't tell me that.

*Why? Why didn't they tell you that?*

Well, I didn't care because I was moving out anyway. But a lot of people didn't want to move.

*When did you move out of the place? And who moved with you?*

Just myself. In 1939. I moved to Birtle, about seven miles north of here.

*Your wife, and your . . . .*

My family, yes. I had my family, too.

*And your eight children.*

Well, I didn't have eight at that time. I only had six.

*Six children.*

Seven.

*And of course your grandfather died in 1933. So there was just your family you moved. And you moved to the railroad house?*

Yes.

*Okay, so when you moved, what did you leave behind? Any cattle?*

No. No, I didn't have any cattle. No.

*You had a building, though.*

Yes. I had the house and the stable, and a little storage shed. Three log buildings.

*And what happened to those buildings?*

They were burned down.

*By whom? Did you see them burned down?*

No. Later, I saw them burnt, but I don't know who set fire to them.

*And is this what happened to all the homes?*

Not all. Some people took some of the homes for firewood and that.

*Why didn't you take it for firewood?*

Well, it was no good to me. I wasn't going to move it 40 miles for firewood when I had lots right at the door.

*Were you upset at the time?*

Oh, not at all.

*So, are you saying that Ste. Madeleine came to the end of its rope? There was no future for it?*

There was no future for it, except for some of the people. In a way, I was frustrated because they didn't treat them right and because the people didn't want to move.

*Where did all these people go?*

Some of the them moved into a place they called Selby Town in the Silver Creek area. Some of them moved into a place they called Fouillard's Corner. Some went up north to Winnipegosis and Crane River and to other different places. They were moving all over.

*Did they all get $150?*

I don't know. No, no, not all. Some of them didn't get anything. The ones who moved down here had log houses built by the municipality. The municipality told them they could build there and stay there for the rest of their lives.

*But that didn't turn out to be the case. Why not?*

Well, the people didn't want to stay there because there was no work around. So they moved away. A lot of them moved into Winnipeg. A lot of them moved to different places, some to Saskatchewan. They're all spread out now.

*So what should they have done?*

Well, if they wanted to stay there, they'd be surrounded by a barbed wire fence, with a yard just big enough for the houses. And they were told that they couldn't take any firewood or use any hay out of the pasture unless they paid a permit for it. And pay for the wood. And they couldn't do that. And that's how they were, we said, forced out. They were not pushed out by force, but they were pushed out because they would be forced to stay in a little lot just the size of the house.

*Well, what should have been done in those days to make the people happier? What could have been done?*

Well, they could have left a couple of sections of land for the people to own a milk cow or a team of horses or something, and live there. But they didn't have to surround each house like they were going to. We went down to St. Lazare and we wanted them to let the people live in the same area.

*Now, I remember coming across a piece of remembrance from somebody who said that the cemetery which occupies two acres of land was supposed to have been five acres, but they didn't keep their promise and they only gave you two acres. Is that true?*

Yes. Yes, there was supposed to be about five acres but the church was there at the time, so they had to leave enough room for people to park near the church, inside the fence. They had fenced that. But then the priest in St. Lazare sold the church and it was supposed to be moved there, somewhere in St. Lazare.

*But it wasn't his to sell.*

No, it wasn't his to sell. It wasn't his bell either. That was our bell. The community bought it, but he took it and sold it just the same.

*The priest did? What was his name?*

I forget his name. I can't think of his name . . . his name is there, but I can't think of it.

*Do you remember that priest?*

Oh, I remember him.

*What kind of a guy was he?*

Oh, I didn't like him.

*Why?*

Because he shouldn't have done that without seeing the people about what they wanted to do, the ones that kept the church. We told him that we didn't want to tear down the church or to spoil anything off the church because we were going to bury our people there.

*This was when? In 1939?*

In 1939, 1940.

*So he sold the church for a piggery.*

Yes.

*But the piggery was not going to be where the church was?*

No. Oh no. They were going to tear it down and move the logs and the roof to where the people had the pigs, down somewhere to the east, southeast of St. Lazare.

*Did he succeed in doing it?*

No, no. We didn't let him do it.

*How come? Tell me the story.*

Well, it was sold and he collected the money.

*How much money?*

I don't know how much he got. He didn't want to tell us. But the money was paid to him. I believe it was around $80 or $90.

*Including the bell?*

Well, the bell was gone then. He had taken the bell already. And all the statues that we had, statues over three feet high. And there were three or four of them. Well, they were all gone, and all the stuff in the church was gone. So when we heard that the church was going to be torn down, we went down to St. Lazare. There's three of us who went down: Norbert Boucher, that's Lena Fleury's father; and John Vermette, that's Caroline's husband; and myself. We went down there and we met the priest in St. Lazare, right on Main Street.

He said he sold it, and I says "Where's the money?"

"Well," he says, "I put it in for the church here."

I says, "Well, that's not fair. You took all our belongings, the bell, all the belongings of the church. You sold them all. The bell's gone east and some other stuff's gone somewhere else. Well, the church is not moving." I said that myself.

I says, "There's two guys that are good shots, and they've got good rifles. The first person that goes and tears the first shingle off that church, he's going to be shot down."

And I says, "Make sure that he goes there pretty seriously, because we're going to be there with rifles. Nobody is going to touch it."

We walked away. And we went out there the next day, when they come there. They didn't touch the church.

*Who were they?*

Well, I don't know. Three guys came to tear down the church. They were hired, I suppose, by the guy that bought it. I don't know who they were. But there were three guys who came with a big truck. They were going to load up the logs, I guess, and whatever they could get, but they never touched it because we were going to shoot them down.

*So what happened?*

They left it, and we moved a family in there to pass the winter there to look after the church. To keep the church.

*What year was this?*

In 1940, I believe. The fall of 1940.

*What family?*

Vermette. Caroline and John Vermette lived there with their family. They had four kids. We moved them there and they didn't have transportation of any kind, so we used to get their groceries for them, help them out, you know, to live there, to hold the church down. That's what we did.

*Did the builders come again? During the winter?*

No, no, no. Not again. They came once, and that was it. They didn't want to take a chance to come anymore.

*They spent the winter of 1940, so it was now 1941. So then what happened to the church, because there's nothing there now?*

Nobody touched it, and then people started taking it, piece by piece. Some of them took a few pieces of lumber from the roof, and somebody else came out and took other parts. We didn't know who they were.

*Were they Metis people?*

I don't know. I don't know who took them. Nobody knew. And there was a little bit of a roof left, and the logs were all there. In this community, which we called the Fouillard's Corner, there was a fellow living there by the name of Boucher . . . .

*A Metis man?*

Gaspard Boucher, yes. He was married to a Fleury sister. He wanted to build a house.

   Well, I said, "Listen, there are only logs, and a little bit of the lumber left from the church. Your house burned down and you can't buy anything. We'll give you a hand and we'll tear it down, move the logs, and build a house with it."

   And we did. So we knew where that went.

*What happened to the pews in the church?*

They were sold. They were taken away by the priest in St. Lazare.

*So the Ste. Madeleine Church was built in 1913 and lasted until 1941?*

Yes. Yes, that was the time that they started taking it apart so we couldn't use it. And then after a while, it was disappearing all of this time. So I gave it to this guy who used the logs. I went to talk to the people first. I asked quite a few of them. I told them the situation and I said, "We'll give them the church and he can use the logs. And at least, we'll know where it went."
  So we did.

*When did Ste. Madeleine cease to be? When were all the homes burned down and nothing was left?*

In 1938.

*And when did the cattle come in? What year?*

They came in right away, in 1939.

*And the cattlemen and farmers had to pay for their cattle to graze?*

Yes. I think it was four or five dollars a year for each head.

*And where did the money go? Who took the money?*

Nobody knew. I don't know. I couldn't tell you where it went. It was supposed to go to the municipality because it came from farmers.

*One of the people says that they came and shot her dogs. Do you know, is that true? They just shot their dogs dead right there?*

Yes, they did. They left them there, you know. But then after 1942, they passed a bylaw that nobody was allowed to keep more than one dog. And if it ran around, they had permission to come and shoot that dog. They claimed that they were killing calves and sheep, you know, and they came to my place, and I had just started working, that was in the fall of '42 or '43. And they came there and I had two dogs, a small one that was in the house all the time, and a big one.

*Who were they?*

The men from the municipality, the councillors. John Dupont was one of them and Gaston Cadieux was one of them. They're dead now. They came to shoot my dog. I walked out of the house with my gun and I said, "Go ahead and shoot him. You're not walking out of here after you shoot him. I got my gun, too."

I was going to shoot them. So they left the dog and they went away. And the cops come.

*The Mounties?*

Oh yes. Well, they just asked me what was the trouble. And I told them. I says, "Anybody that's going to shoot that dog in there without my permission, he gets shot."

I says, "And I mean it." That got it settled.

Oh, yeah. Yeah, they shot quite a few dogs because people had a couple of dogs, you know, two or three, some of them. Because they were using them for sleigh dogs, you see. That was late in 1942, 1943, you know, after I came home from the sanitorium.

*Do you think that the Metis people, about 260 all together, who lived there, should get some form of compensation today, 48 years later?*

Well, that's the way I feel.

*What should they get?*

I think that people should be compensated in one way or the other. I don't mean to say in cash money or anything, but I think that they should be. They should be compensated one way that will be usable for them, you know. Like there's a lot of people that are still poor. They haven't got nothing. They didn't work like I did. I was lucky. But there's a lot of them that didn't know that work and couldn't make any more money than barely a living.

*Should these Metis people or their families get money or land today? If Premier Howard Pawley were here or Prime Minister Brian Mulroney were here, what would you ask for?*

Well, you can't ask for land because land is mostly all occupied. They can't go and take land that is owned by other people and give it to the Metis people. But I think they should be compensated somehow. They should be looked after in different ways, for the rest of their lives. So a person would have to look into that. And the government should compensate these Metis people. Since the days of their ancestors they've lost everything. They been pushed around here and there and to different places. I think that they should be compensated for their lives. But to tell you which way, I couldn't say. I would have to sit down with the planners to plan these things, to settle things without having too much difficulty.

*Do you feel a crime was done to the Metis people of Ste. Madeleine?*

Well, in a sort of way, yes. In a sort of way. They shouldn't have been pushed out of there because, you know, it was their homes. They felt as if they were killed. They felt that they were dead. They had no home. They felt that they had no place to go. They would be just like a dog. You throw a dog out and it just, it feels that way. That's the way they feel.

*And they still feel that way today?*

They still feel that way today. They still feel that they were pushed out of there for nothing. Just like animals, you know. That's the way they feel. I've talked to them a lot of times. And a lot of them don't mind, but lots of them feel that they shouldn't have been treated that way. They should be compensated by the government. They've been pushed, from years back, hundreds of years back, in fact.

*How long have the Metis people been living in Ste. Madeleine?*

Oh, I couldn't answer that. I don't know how long, but they had been there for many years, in the 1800s.

*I'd like you to comment on this. In 1921, you bought 80 acres of land you registered in your grandfather's name because you were underage. You paid $400 for it and you paid the taxes until 1929. After 1929, you couldn't afford to pay the taxes, so effectively, you were squatting on the land.*

Yes.

*So when you left in 1939, which was ten years later, all you got was $150 or $17 a month until it was paid. But the provisions of the PFRA were that if you had paid your taxes, year by year, they would have transported your cattle, if you had any, to another location, and they would have given you a similar amount of land.*

Amount of land, yes.

*But you weren't entitled to that?*

No, no.

*You knew that? You were told that clearly?*

Yes.

*And were the other Metis people told that clearly, too?*

Yes, they were. They knew, the ones that understood. But lots of them didn't understand. The majority didn't understand.

*Because they didn't have the education?*

They didn't have the education.

*To them, they were just being pushed off the land.*

Pushed off, that's how they felt. That's just the way they think it happened. I didn't feel that way because I understood what they were doing. In fact, I went to them and said, "If you're going to build a pasture there, the Metis people should have a chance to work on it."
    We were hired, the ones able to work, able to do the work they were required to do. I worked there.

*Yesterday, when I spoke to George Ducharme, he said he worked on building the pasture in 1937, making picket fences and that. Somebody squealed on him because he was underaged, and he got off that. He says that there was a lot of jealousy.*

Yes. [Laughs] Yes, I worked on there. We cut the lines and dug for post holes and marked the land.

*But it was a small amount of work for a short time.*

Just a short time. In fact, I only worked there for about two weeks.

*Do you remember what you got paid?*

No, I don't. [Laughs] But not much.

*Going back to 1918, when you were twelve, I believe you were staying with your grandfather, your grandmother and their children, and there was this terrible flu epidemic.*

Yes.

*And people died, including people in your family. Can you go through that again? Can you tell me that story again?*

Yes. We were all living . . . we had moved into St. Lazare. We had our home over there.

*Why weren't you in Ste. Madeleine?*

Well, because we had to work near St. Lazare. We moved there to be able to work. At that time, we had to transport with horses and it took a long time to travel 30 miles. We had work not too far from Lazare so we moved into a house to be closer. And that's the time that the flu came out. That was at the end of the war, and it came out in the fall. After the harvesting was all done, people started to get sick. I never got sick. I was the only one that didn't get sick. My uncle was working for a farmer when his wife took sick. So he moved his children into our home, at my grandfather's place. And in a few days, they sent her body by train from Winnipeg.

*What were their names?*

She was a Houle. Marie, I think. So we had to go and pick up her coffin from the train and bring her home. Of course, it was only about a mile. And my uncle had the flu. He didn't even know his wife had already died. He was unconscious. and the next night, his little boy died. He was about five years old.

*This was in your house in St. Lazare?*

Yes. This was in our house in St. Lazare.

*Is that house still around?*

No, it's torn down.

*So what happened? Tell me more.*

Well, he had two girls. They were about eight and nine years old, and they both died in one night. He didn't even know about it. And the next night, my grandmother died. Nobody knew about it but me. I was the only one up.

*So what did you do?*

I had to move them into a cold place. We had a back kitchen we weren't using. I had to drag the body of my aunt across the floor, out there and cover her with a sheet. And I had to drag the body of my grandmother, and she was a woman who weighed about 200 pounds, but she wasn't that fat when she died. I had to drag her along, across the front room and across the kitchen, into the back kitchen, where I laid them on the floor and covered them with sheets.

*You were twelve at the time.*

Yes. And the two little girls and the boy, I carried them into that place and laid them all on the floor in a row. And they were all covered there.

*How long were they there?*

Oh, they were there quite a few days. They were there four or five days, about a week, before they could get buried.

*Why did they have to stay there that long?*

There were too many dying. There was a pile of coffins, a pile up in the cemetery. Thirteen, fourteen, seventeen coffins piled up in there, people bringing them in. They couldn't dig fast enough to bury them all. So when they got them buried, they came and picked up the two girls and the boy and my aunt and my grandmother, and they buried them all in one grave. A big grave, that was. They dug a big grave and they buried them there. There was six buried in one grave.

*In coffins?*

Oh yeah, they had coffins. They brought coffins for them.

*Who paid for the coffins?*

I don't know. There wasn't anything mentioned.

*Was this the first time you had encountered dead people?*

No. Of course I wasn't very old, but I saw dead people before. Well, there's a lot of times that people were by themselves and you'd go there when a person died and you knew that you had to help. I'd help, you know. Before. A couple of times.

*To do what?*

Change clothes off the dead people. Wash them.

*When you were twelve and younger?*

Yes. Oh, I was younger. Younger than that even.

*So you were used to touching dead people?*

Oh yes. And I'd built coffins.

*When you were how old?*

About twelve, thirteen years old. And then all along, until 1937. I don't know how many coffins I built. I built lots of them.

*When you had to deal with your dead grandmother and all the other people who died, in your house in St. Lazare, did it affect you? Were you in tears? Were you upset?*

No, you couldn't be in tears, because if you were, you couldn't do anything like that. No. I just made up my mind that I was going to look after them. And I made up my mind that I was not going to cry. Because if I had cried, I would have never done it. I stood it, you know. I had to get them out.

*Before they died, did you feed them?*

Yes, I fed them.

*How? What?*

I fed them by spoon. I used to boil meat. And the doctor gave me a bottle of whiskey. I can't tell you what kind of whiskey it was. But he brought a big bottle of whiskey and he said when you make broth out of meat, put it in a cup or a glass, and put so much whiskey in it and feed them to the sick ones. And I fed my uncle that way, and my aunt, my grandfather, and my brother. And these other people that died, I fed them that way. By spoon.

*Did you have time to sleep?*

Very little. Very little because I'd just fall asleep and somebody would call.

*When you tell me this story, and I think about how old you were, you were just a baby, you were twelve years old, and when I see children today, twelve years old, they don't have to do these things.*

No, no.

*Their lifestyle is so different. They have fun, they have games, they can play. Do you think you grew up too fast?*

I don't know. But it's just as I told you before, I was a man at twelve. I worked to earn a living for a family, at twelve. Right after the flu, I had to work because my grandfather got so bad that time, his health never returned. And he couldn't earn a living for me. I didn't have a chance to think about anything, you know. That's the reason why I never went to school.

*So somewhere along these 79 years that you have lived, what did you do for fun? How did you relax? How do you catch up on those years when you were a little boy and then you became a man all at once, and you had no chance to play? No chance to play hockey, to bowl, do all those things? How have you made up for it since?*

The only thing that I did is to get along with the people and have friends. I could go talk to them and have fun with them by playing pool or playing cards, things like that. That's the only pleasure I had. All the way across, I never had too much chance to go and join anything, you know, like socials of any kind. But after I got old enough, when I was sixteen, I became a dancer. I'd dance all night, you know. I used to like dances. That's the only pleasure, the only recreation that we had at that time.

*If you could have the power to impress people, how would you like people to remember you when you're gone? What would you like them to think about you?*

Well, I don't know . . . but I think that they'd think of me as a friend, you know. Because I was friendly with all people. Now, if they thought of me like that, I'd be very glad. I'd be a happy man. Because I never hurt anybody . . . I don't think I've hurt anybody's feelings, and I think that they'd think of me as, you know, an honest man. I never cheated anybody. I never beat anybody out of anything. And I was a great help to a lot of people.

*And still are.*

And still are. I think they would think of me as a man who, you know, who helped a lot of people. And I still do. Because I think when a person needs help, you don't have to look at friendship. Whether he's your friend or not, if he needs help, he needs help. I did a lot of things for people. Lots of times. Lots of times. Even when I was only sixteen, seventeen years old.

*I think it's time for us to call it a day. Joe Venne, thank you.*

Thank you very much.

*ALEXANDRE VENNE, 1919*
*(Joe Venne's father)*
*Photo was taken in Portage la
Prairie, prior to his second marriage
to Philomene Ducharme of St.
Ambroise. Mr. Venne sent this
photo to his children in Ste.
Madeleine. The Venne family was
originally from North Dakota.*

*EARLY RESIDENTS OF STE.
MADELEINE VISIT RUSSELL FAIR, 1922
L-R, standing: Cecile Bellehumeur (daughter
of Pat Bellehumeur and Joe Venne's cousin),
William John Fleury (Joe Venne's uncle).
L-R, sitting: Véronique Fisher (Joe Venne's
aunt and his mother's sister), Helen Fleury
(nee Smith, wife of William J. Fleury),
Baptiste Fleury (Joe Venne's grandfather).*

*THRESHING TIME, 1924*
*Joe Venne, age 17, operating a threshing machine in the fall of 1924,
on George Fowler's farm, three miles northwest of Binscarth.*

78

### STE. MADELEINE WEDDING PARTY, 1926

*L-R: Josephine Vermette (Joe Venne's future wife), Alcid Flammand (son of Alex Flammand), Alice Bellehumeur (daughter of Pat Bellehumeur, brother-in-law of Louis Riel), Joe Venne, Bernadette Fisher (daughter of Ambroise and Véronique Fisher), Felix Fleury (son of John Fleury), Caroline Vermette (daughter of Ambroise and Véronique Fisher), and John Vermette (son of Alec Vermette).*

*The photo was taken on John and Caroline Vermette's wedding day, northwest quarter of Section 29, Ste. Madeleine.*

### HAULING WATER, 1939

*Mrs. George Laycock took this picture of Joe Venne, age 33, and his oldest daughter, Olive, age 10, in the winter of 1939, on the Laycock farm in the Foxwarren district, where Joe worked as a labourer.*

*RESIDENTS OF STE. MADELEINE, CHRISTMAS 1927*

*L-R standing: Joe Boucher (Agnes Boucher's husband), Ernestine Venne (Joe Venne's sister),
Mary Fleury (Joe Venne's aunt on his mother's side), Katherine Bellehumeur (cousin of Joe Venne),
Adele Fleury (Joe Venne's aunt on his mother's side), and Joe Venne, age 21.
Sitting: Isadore Venne, age 17 (Joe Venne's brother).*

## AGNES BOUCHER

*Agnes Côté was born July 6, 1912, in Welby, Saskatchewan, to Joseph Côté and Elizabeth (nee) Pritchard. Her mother died in childbirth, and Agnes moved in with her grandparents, Edward Pritchard and Marie (nee) Desjarlais. The Pritchard family, originally from St. Francois Xavier (near Winnipeg) had moved to Welby in the early 1900s to work on the railroad.*

*Agnes attended Welby School up to grade eight. In 1930, she married Joseph Boucher and moved with him to Ste. Madeleine where his family had been settled for several generations. They lived on Section 32, near the Ste. Madeleine church, where they farmed and raised cattle and chickens. In 1932, the post office was set up in their house, where it remained until 1941. After the community pasture was set up, the Bouchers were able to exchange their land for new acreage in the Assiniboine Valley. They later moved to the Banana Belt district, where they farmed up until 1973, when their son took over the land. Joe Boucher passed away in December, 1985.*

*Agnes continues to live in Binscarth where she loves to garden. She visits often with her thirteen children and their families, many of whom also live in the Binscarth area.*

*Joe Venne was present during her interview.*

*Mrs. Boucher, can you tell me when you first moved to Ste. Madeleine?*

In 1930. December 30 was the day I was married. And that's when I moved in.

*Were you married in Ste. Madeleine?*

No, I was married in my hometown of Welby, Saskatchewan.

*And then you moved from Welby directly?*

Directly.

*Did you get to Ste. Madeleine that day?*

Yes.

*Tell me about the day of the wedding, how you actually travelled.*

Well, we used the horse and a car. Some of the bridal party came in my uncle's 1928 Ford. We went by horse. We didn't have the road that he was travelling on. We just had trails. He came across the Welby plains which you could cross almost anywhere because there was hardly any snow then. That was the year the drought started. We lived with my father-in-law for the first year. In the second year, the following spring, we moved on our own to the Lemay place where my husband had rented a half-section. And from there on, we raised two children. After the second one came, we had the post office for, I guess, ten years. We used to transport the mail from Binscarth, by horse and buggy, every Friday. In wintertime, it would be the same thing, we'd either use a cutter or a sleigh, a team and sleigh to bring the mail home. And that mail was distributed every Friday.

*How was it distributed? Did you go from door to door, or people came to you?*

No, the people came to our door and got their mail.

*What did a letter cost in those days?*

I think it was two cents.

*Anywhere in Canada?*

Yes.

*You got to Ste. Madeleine in 1930. Did you know what you were going into, what it would be like?*

Well, I had a general idea, yes. It seemed that in the '30s, everybody was in the same boat. Nobody had any money. Nobody had anything. We just lived on whatever money we could make. We had, I think, four cows to start with, a few chickens and a few horses. That's what we had to start with. And between Joe and his father, we managed to farm the half section of land that we had.

*Now, this half section of land, was it within Ste. Madeleine?*

Yes, it was.

*And did you pay taxes on the land?*

Yes, we did.

*And you paid them right up to the end?*

Yes.

*Now, Mrs. Boucher, the reason I asked you whether you paid taxes, was that in 1935, the PFRA came in across western Canada. And the provisions of that act said that where pasturelands were to be created, the government was obliged to pay the people, by giving them transport for their animals off the land. Also they would give them an equal amount of land, outside of the land that had been fenced in. Were you made aware of that?*

Not at that particular time. But we were made aware in 1939, that the community pasture was coming in and that we had to find another place to move. That's when we bought this other place in this valley, from a man by the name of Mr. Victor.

*Okay, you say that you first found out in 1939. How did you find out? Who told you and what did they tell you?*

Well, it was a municipal clerk that came up and told us.

*What was his name?*

Mr. Selby. John Selby.

*And what did he tell you?*

He told us that we'd have to move out from there and go elsewhere to make our living. And he had moved a lot of families from there, as well, and placed them wherever they could find work.

*What rights did you have then? Did he outline the rights you had as a taxpayer who owned a half section of land?*

Yes. We just made a trade with them and got the valley.

*You got 320 acres there? And was it a good trade?*

Yes.

*Now why did you have to move from Ste. Madeleine?*

Because of the community pasture. The government had taken it all.

*Do you know why they did it? Do you know the reasons behind it?*

No, I don't.

*Now, were you given money to transport your cattle from one part to the other? Or was that unnecessary?*

That was unnecessary. We didn't have to go that far. It was about three miles from where we were.

*Now the other thing was, when you heard that you had to move from Ste. Madeleine, when you and your husband and family were there, what kind of conversations took place among yourselves?*

Well, at that time, we were quite happy to go elsewhere because the land we were getting was a lot better than what we had before.

*What was wrong with the land you already had?*

It was very sandy. The land that we got was very good land.

*And does your family still own that land?*

Yes, we do.

*And what do they do with that land?*

They still cultivate it. They're still seeding. They grow mostly whatever grain is most popular, like sometimes most of it is wheat, barley or oats.

*Were there any other families, in the same position as yourself, who had paid their taxes, who weren't squatting?*

No, there wasn't.

*How many people lived in Ste. Madeleine, to the best of your recollection at that time?*

There were about twenty families.

*And how many people would that be?*

They all had big families. I just can't say offhand.

*Just throw out a figure that is approximately right.*

Oh, I'd say about 150.

*So you're saying that of all the twenty families, the only family that was able to pay their taxes, during this hardship period and, thus, fell into the requirements of the PFRA, was the Boucher family?*

Yes.

*And all the rest were kicked off the land?*

Yes.

*Now you understood that quite well?*

Yes.

*But in talking to some of the people who were kicked off the land, they seemed to not have understood that well. There is an underlying resentment, a feeling that they were picking on the Metis people, the poor people. In fact, only one person, so far, indicated that he got any kind of money, a very small amount, but most of the others got nothing. Do you think there was a communication problem? That they never informed the people properly?*

I think so, myself. I remember there were a lot of families who could have done better but since they couldn't prop themselves up, it seems that they were always let down in a lot of ways. If anybody was willing to go ahead and plot for themselves, they got more pull, it seems, than those who were lazy. Some were just squatters and didn't seem to care. That's the way I looked at it anyways. As far as our land there, we had to pay something. I can't remember, offhand, how much we had to pay, but we did have to give something to the municipality.

*This was for the original piece in Ste. Madeleine?*

No, the piece of land in the valley.

*The piece in the valley, that you got afterwards. Right. But this was what the PFRA said you must get. So, it was part of the government swap. What do you think the government could have done to have helped the Metis people, the other nineteen families that were there?*

Maybe if they were given each a little piece of land and helped along. Maybe they would have done something. I know that a lot of them were quite angry about it. They almost rebelled. They didn't want to leave the bit of possessions they had there.

*And do you think that it was wrong that they had to go?*

Well, in a way I don't because once the government took it over, what could they do there? They couldn't live on that plot because there was nothing there for them to do.

*Did the government give them any alternatives? They talk about Fouillard's Corner and Selby Town . . . .*

Well, the reason they're called that is because, at that time, Mr. Ben Fouillard was the councillor, and Mr. Selby was the secretary-treasurer of the municipality. And anytime they wanted relief, those were the two men they went to. And of course, some of them didn't want to go abroad, like some went to Ste. Rose and Oak River, up north. And then a few families stayed. They didn't want to go. So that's how come they were squatting in that valley there which they now call Selby Town. And a lot of them stayed near where the church is now. There were a few families who stayed outside the community. That was called Fouillard's Corner. Some from the reserve were able to stay there, too.

*When you say, from the reserve, do you mean Indian people? There were some Indian people who also lived in Ste. Madeleine?*

Yes. It was all mixed, you see. But they couldn't live on the reserve. The reserve was separated from their little squatting area.

*Yes, in fact, I've been to Fouillard's Corner, and it's right across the street from the Indian reserve. So there's a kind of mixture there.*

There's a separation there.

*So was Selby Town and Fouillard's Corner an interim measure, where some of the people from Ste. Madeleine could go, if they didn't want to go to Alberta, Saskatchewan or northern Manitoba?*

Yes. They just stayed there and never went.

*And the council of the municipality of Ellice allowed them to squat?*

They allowed them to squat and helped them with their provisions during the winter. But some of the people went out to work in the summertime, as much as they could, to try and find more income.

*Now, Mrs. Boucher, the land was made into common pastureland. What happened to it then? Were cattle brought in to graze?*

Yes.

*Do you know how much money it cost to graze your cattle there?*

No, I don't because we never had to put our cattle in there ourselves. We had enough pasture.

*And who used it?*

It was mostly outsiders from different towns. There were some from Russell, Binscarth, Birtle, from all over, who used the pasture.

*And people just leave their cattle there?*

They just leave them there and then they have to pay so much a head for letting them graze there.

*And who did they pay the money to?*

To the community pasture manager.

*Was that a federal, provincial or municipal authority?*

It must have went to whoever was the head of it.

*I talked to about a half dozen people who had been squatters and had left Ste. Madeleine, and not one left my company without tears in his eyes and this is 48 years later. For every single one, the memory is as vivid as if it happened yesterday. It was like the destruction of their lives because from that point on, they were pushed and shoved and they've been everywhere. Why is there this terrible upset?*

Oh, I guess they were so used to being together. They didn't want to be separated. It's just like us; if we have a circle of people, well, when we have to leave, when everyone has to go their separate ways, naturally, we don't feel good about it.

*Do you sympathize with what happened to those people?*

Yes. I do, yes.

*And how can that problem be solved today? If you had a magic wand and could do it, what would you do?*

Well, first of all, I'd see that they had good lodging, that they'd be comfortable. And see that they had three meals a day. And help them out in any way they need help. Because a lot of them haven't got the education. They don't know what's going on. They're just told things by word of mouth, from somebody, and half the time it's not the truth.

*Back in 1937, 1938, when the surveyors first started to come in, what happened then?*

I think what happened then, they promised them better things which didn't mature.

*What were some of those promises? Do you remember?*

Well, a lot of them had told me when they used to come for their mail: "We're supposed to be moving out from here and we're going to be given better homes and we'll have a better living where they're going to take us."
    And I asked one fellow, where. "Well, they're going to take us to the Red Lakes where we can fish and have all the fish we want and where there's game."

*Who was that fellow?*

It was Mr. Ducharme, Pete Ducharme.

*And other people, did they tell you similar stories?*

Yes.

*So who gave these promises to the people?*

It must have been whoever was approaching them to get them to move out. I wouldn't say in particular who they were. But I think it was mostly the municipality that was involved in it, like the municipal clerks and that.

*I should add that the PFRA pastures were established not only in Ste. Madeleine, but right across the prairies. It was not an act designed to push the Metis people out. It was an act designed to protect the land.*

Yes.

*But the question is, since this was a federal act, how did the municipality get involved because there were no federal agents? Were there not people from Ottawa or from Winnipeg involved?*

Oh, there could have been people who came and asked the municipality to do this. I don't know.

*Now, you kept your post office in Ste. Madeleine until 1942, right?*

No, it wasn't quite 1942 because we moved in 1941, to our homestead in the valley. That's when we had to disband with the rest of them and close the post office.

*What month? Do you remember?*

When we moved, it was spring.

*So when you left in spring of 1941, were there any families still there?*

Yes, there were four or five families still there. Later, they moved to Selby Town.

*And did the people from the PFRA do anything? I heard stories of houses being burned, of a church being made into a pigsty, and of dogs being shot. Can you talk about that?*

Well, I know that during the time they were living there, there was a Dupont. They used to call him the dog-eater. [Laughs] He used to come up and get rid of those dogs because they had too many of them. The poor dogs were starving.

*So he was from the municipality and he . . . .*

He was from St. Lazare.

*St. Lazare. And was he a Metis person?*

No.

*He wasn't. So there was friction there?*

There was friction, of course, for they didn't like their dogs to get killed, naturally. I mean, he used to kill the dogs.

*Did the Metis women of Ste. Madeleine mix with other communities?*

No, not much.

*So they had no real knowledge of what was going on in the villages, how people thought, and so on? Can you comment on this?*

Well, the Metis didn't mix because it seemed that everywhere they went, they were treated as the lower-class person.

*And what about the men?*

Well, I'm sure the men felt the same way, too, but they had to get out and do something about it. It was very seldom that the women went out, even to go to town to shop.

*How did they do their shopping then?*

Mostly, the men did it. When they'd come home on the weekends, they'd bring the provisions.

*In one conversation I had with one woman, she said she only had six years education because they couldn't go to school. They didn't have shoes sometimes.*

Yes. That's true.

*And I guess they were just so cold, they couldn't go to school. So this was poverty.*

This was poverty, the way they were.

*Was there any help, like welfare, against this poverty, in those days?*

Well, at that time, they just called it relief. And there was a Dr. Gilbart who used to come from Spy Hill and he used to bring whatever clothes he could find to fit those kids. Most of the time things would come to our place there, at the post office. He'd be there and he'd have the families come over and fit them with whatever he had. And at Christmas time, there'd always be Christmas cheer, like he'd bring toys and candies for them.

*I've heard remarkable stories about this man.*

Oh, he was wonderful.

*Tell me about him.*

He used to come to the sick, no matter if he had to come on snowshoes or walk, or whatever, he would get there. If his car didn't make it, he would walk the rest of the way. And his stopping place would be at my house. He'd come in and say, "Now Agnes, have you got the kettle on?"
   "Yes."
   "Have you got a piece of bread for me?"
   "Yes."
   "What about some hot soup or something?"
   Well, I'd make him some hot soup. And he'd carry on from there and go the rest of the way.

*What motivated him?*

He felt sorry for the families. He came from the north. I can't remember where now. He used to talk Saulteaux. He was with the Indians, maybe in Crane River, that area. And that's how he felt. He should be with them.

*Was he a god-fearing man?*

Yes. He was a strong believer.

*And the people liked him. Did they pay him?*

No. There was no pay.

*So who paid him?*

He just got it out of whoever he could. And he had his own pharmacy. Whatever he could make for them to get better, he would bring it to them.

*And what was his full name?*

F.O. Gilbart. Frank Oliver, I think.

*Do you remember when he died?*

He died at the coast. I'd say in the 1960s, about 20 years ago. We went to visit him one year, when he was in Vancouver.

*Did he have a family?*

Yes, he had a boy and a girl. They must still be there. I can't remember the boy's name but I remember Jean very well.

*About health, what did people do if one had a toothache?*

They all had good teeth. They didn't have what we do nowadays. It's all these additives that we have nowadays that's rotting our teeth and our systems. [Laughs] They had the plain food, and I think that's what was best for each one of us.

*Was there a lot of folk medicine?*

Well, whatever they could make, I guess. Yes, there was a lot.

*Who practised it?*

Just whatever they could hear from one another. If they told you that mint tea was good for anybody who had a cold . . . they'd drink a lot of that. And there were wild herbs that they used to dig. Especially Mrs. Smith, she was very good at gathering herbs. And there was also a midwife, Mrs. Bercier. She was very good, especially for women ailments. I had her for seven of my children.

*You had seven of your children delivered by a midwife? So how many did you have all together?*

I had thirteen children.

*Thirteen children. Are they all alive?*

Yes. I nearly died with the seventh one. I was very, very sick. And we lived on a farm in the valley and we didn't have a phone . . . .

*What year was that?*

That was in 1942.

*This was the year after you'd moved from Ste. Madeleine?*

Yes. And we didn't have a phone, so my husband forded the river with the horse, across to the nearest phone. At that time, Jack MacDougall lived there. He phoned Binscarth for Dr. Torrance, but he was gone to Clear Lake. We couldn't get him. So he phoned one from Birtle and he was away on a case. So Joe just came home. And by that time, the midwife had saved both of us.

And after that, she said, "I will never look after you again because I've had too many problems with this seventh child of yours." [Laughs]

So then after that, we moved to the farm on top of the hill there, where my son is living now, and I went to the hospital in Russell for the rest of my babies and had a doctor tend to me.

*Was Mrs. Bercier a Metis person?*

Yes.

*And where did she live?*

She lived in Ste. Madeleine where the rest of us were when we had the post office. That's where she lived.

*But this was 1942. Where was she in 1942?*

She was living in Fouillard's Corner, not far from there. She delivered 250 babies.

*Today, it's quite common when a baby's born, for the husband to watch the delivery. Was your husband present for any of the births?*

No. My husband was never near my bedroom for any of my babies. He would be outside somewhere, or somewhere nearby and they would call him.

*Now, 48 years later, after Ste. Madeleine is leveled, and the cattle graze there every summer, only the cemetery remains, two acres instead of the promised five. Its crosses are falling over and it's a little weedy and wet and grassy. Nevertheless, there is something there. What are your feelings now? Do you visit Ste. Madeleine?*

Yes. And my thoughts and feelings are very sad. I feel those, who have souls lying there, should really look after it. I don't think it should be an outsider. I think it should be their own people who should do it.

*And what about the ruins there? There are outlines of the church, the old school, Belliveau School, and stones where buildings and houses used to be. Do they echo to you? Do they talk to you when you go over the ground?*

Oh yes. They give me memories of when I used to have the post office and when I used to walk to the school with Rosalie when she first started kindergarten. I used to have the teachers boarding at our house. It wasn't called kindergarten then but the teacher used to say, "This afternoon, perhaps you can send Rosalie up to come play with the kids, so she gets used to school."

*Now, you were in Ste. Madeleine for eleven years, do you remember who the teachers were at Belliveau School during that period?*

Well, there was Albert Lecote. He's still living in St. Boniface, I think. Others were Mary Maisson from Ste. Rose, a Miss Lussier from St. Leon . . . and Denis St. Onge. And Leon Frechette, he's still in St. Boniface. He was there for about three years.

*Now can you tell me what was the quality of education? First of all did you send your own kids there?*

No. Because they were too young. We sent our kids to Gambler School. There was an English girl who was teaching there and there were a lot of English people.

*So why didn't you send your kids to Belliveau School?*

Because that's when the place was all demolished and there was nothing there. I had to send them to Gambler's. Gambler was about two miles away and they had to ford the Assiniboine River. In the spring, when the river was high, we always crossed them with a little raft. And when it got too high, Rosalie stayed with the Coxes and the two boys, Elmer and George, stayed at Jack MacDougall's.

*This was after 1941?*

Yes, after 1941. And there's one time in 1943, that the river was high and they were crossing on this raft. The rope broke and they went sailing down the river. But my husband was calm. He never let on what was going on. Down deep in his mind, he thought maybe he'd never bring them home safely. But he managed to catch a willow and brought them to safety, to the ground. And they came in, I guess it was about eleven o'clock, with all their lunch pails and everything else, and Rosalie came in and grabbbed me.

She had a speech impediment. She stuttered. "Mom, we pretty nearly drowned," she said. "Daddy couldn't get the raft to go across the river because the rope broke and our pole wasn't long enough to reach the bottom of the river."

And I said, "What did you do?"

"Nothing. We were just happy. We were floating along." [Laughs]

*It's a good thing you weren't there. Your heart would have been in your throat.*

Yes. Died a thousand deaths.

*Now, let's talk about the church. Was the church important in your life? During the eleven years that you were there?*

Yes.

*How often was the church open? Was there a priest there?*

A priest from St. Lazare used to come every second Sunday.

*Were priests strict about marriage? For instance, if some of the Metis people who lived there were unwed and had children and maybe parted . . . .*

In those days, not many left their husbands because the priests were very, very strict. If any of them lived common-law, they had no right to be in the church.

*So was there a lot of pressure put on the people?*

Yes, there was pressure put on them for that particular subject.

*And did the priests come into the village? Did they walk around and visit the people?*

Oh yes. They visited. They'd come and visit each family.

*Did they stay with you?*

They had their meals with us, yes.

*Now, the priests and the church were an important part of the life, but in 1940, 1941, the church was sold. One of the priests sold the church, and it was made into a pigsty. And some of the Metis people defended it . . . .*

I don't recollect that the church was sold. I can't remember.

*That the bell tower was sold? The bell was taken and shipped to the east and the people weren't consulted?*

I know the bell was taken away, but I had understood at the time, that it was the bishop's order.

*But the bell belonged to the people of the community. They had paid for it out of their own labor. And no one consulted them. And there is lingering resentment among the people even today, about that. Do you remember that?*

**Joe Venne:** I'll have to correct you on that. She wasn't there at the time we bought the bell. That was in about 1924 to 1926.

That's why I have no recollection of that.

**Joe Venne:** We made socials to buy the bell. That's how we bought it. The priests and the parish didn't put anything out. We did. The community.

*Okay, thank you. All right then, you're clearly not aware of the problem that existed about the church building having been sold by the priests at the time in 1941.*

I just took it for granted that it all belonged to the diocese and it had to go back to the bishop, and he could do what he wanted to do with it. That's what I had believed.

*Okay, now, I'm an outsider, but it's very easy to identify with the victims, in the sense that the victims are the Metis people. They were kicked out, one way or another, legally or not; they were without a place to live, after 1939, the 1940s. They were the good guys. Who were the bad guys?*

To my knowledge, I don't think anybody was bad.

*So who is the villain? Why is it that the Metis people are so upset and angry and their memories are so vivid about what happened? If you could point your finger and blame anyone for what took place, who would you blame?*

I can't say who it would be. Because I wasn't in their same situation. I can't say.

*Can you talk about what being Metis means to you?*

Well, to begin with . . . . Is it because they were crossed with the white man and the Indian? That mixture?

*I can't answer that. I'm only asking if the perception of being Metis has a particular meaning to you?*

No, not really . . . .

*What about language? Was there a special language the Metis people spoke that others didn't?*

Well, they spoke a broken Cree. It wasn't the true Cree. It was mixed with French.

*And English?*

Yes, and English.

*What about culture? What was their culture, in terms of music, food and storytelling?*

Oh, they were good storytellers. They were good musicians, good violin players. There was Isadore Venne, Joe's brother, here. And there was Bill Boucher, a cousin of my husband's.

*Did you go to their dances?*

Yes. We used to go to their parties, yes.

*Where were the parties held?*

At the homes.

*In Ste. Madeleine. And were the people friendly?*

Oh, very friendly. That's why I say there wasn't anyone I could say was my enemy. They were all very nice people.

*Was the community life there better than it is today?*

Oh, it was much happier.

*So do you miss that?*

Yes, yes.

**Joe Venne:** You caught the tail end of it.

*You caught the tail end of it, Joe says.*

Yes, that's what they say. But we did have good times together.

*Now talk about the food.*

Their culture was mostly just what they call the bannock. And some bread, of course. A lot of them made bread. But mostly, they would make fresh bannock for each meal.

*If I were to visit you and your family in Ste. Madeleine, what would you serve me, if you had liked me and invited me for supper? What would be an ordinary meal in those days?*

Oh, it'd be chicken, prairie chicken and you could maybe get rabbit. We used to eat a lot of rabbit.

*How would you prepare that?*

In the '30s, I would dress my rabbit, and soak it in salt and water and try to get all the blood out of it. That's one way to get all the blood out of any wild meat, by soaking it in a lot of salt and water. And I would parboil it or roast it or fry it with onions and salt and pepper. And then, if you wanted a stew, I would make it the same way, too. I would brown my meat real good and boil it until it came off the bones.

*Did you serve a lot of vegetables in those days?*

Yes, we did. Mostly, it was carrots and peas and turnips.

*What about green leafy things? And tomatoes?*

Well, we just had tomatoes in the fall because we couldn't get them in the stores like we do nowadays. Lettuce was the same.

*What about fruit?*

Fruit? Well, we used to buy fruit by the case and then just can it for the winter. Because we didn't have facilities like what we have now, such as deep freezers, to put it away when it was fresh.

*Did you use wild berries?*

Yes, a lot. Lot of saskatoons and chokecherries. We used to make a syrup. And cranberries, we made cranberry jelly.

*My mouth is watering. Now we've talked about food and its importance. Was alcohol a problem in Ste. Madeleine, to your knowledge?*

Not really. Not too much.

*Why?*

Well, there weren't too many who could afford to buy the sugar to use in the brew.

*So people would party without too much alcohol?*

They would party without alcohol. Oh no, they didn't need that to party with.

*Somebody I spoke to, said that the parties in Ste. Madeleine could go on until four, five in the morning.*

Oh yes. We'd start about eight o'clock and go until daybreak. I remember one time, we celebrated my husband's birthday because it was always during Lent and he was having a birthday outside of Lent. And they all gathered at our place then. I had a neighbor, Mrs. Vermette, who made chokecherry wine and she made five gallons of it. And of course, that went with the party. It was cold so nobody went home. We were milking cows for breakfast. Everybody went to help milk the cows. We made a great big pot of porridge and everybody had porridge, right before they went home. [Laughs] That was our party!

**Joe Venne:** We had lots of fun that time.

*Well, you make it sound really hospitable. If again, I could be in Ste. Madeleine, could you take me now for a guided tour of your home?*

Well, upstairs, there was . . . .

*You had an upstairs?*

We had an upstairs and a downstairs. And we had a kitchen. Upstairs was divided into two bedrooms. Like it was the whole upstairs but divided into two. They were curtained off.

*Any windows? How many windows upstairs?*

We had two windows at each end of the place.

*And how was the house built?*

With logs.

*And downstairs?*

Downstairs was the same thing. Two rooms.

*Can you tell me where you got your water from?*

We had a well and we just pumped it up by hand.

*And what kind of toilet facilities?*

We had an outdoor toilet.

*And any other outbuildings besides that?*

We had our little milk shed, like an ice house. We used to preserve our ice with sawdust and hay. And that's what kept the cream cool.

*And did you sell your cream?*

Yes. I used to have to take my cream by horse and buggy, three miles to meet the truck, every Friday. And sometimes, if I couldn't make the truck, I would churn that cream and make it into butter. And I would take it to Welby, about six to eight miles from where we lived. I would churn that butter at five in the morning while the sun was still down and by eight o'clock, I was at the store with my butter, all weighed into pounds. I used to get fifteen cents a pound for it.

*Was that good money in those days?*

It was for us. Ten cents a dozen for our eggs. I'd come home with my groceries for the week and be happy.

*So you would have very little money left over.*

Very little. Just have to go from one week to the other.

*Did you have a barn?*

Yes. We milked ten cows, then. We had a chicken coop. We had a team of eight horses to work the land with.

*And what kind of crops did you sow in Ste. Madeleine?*

Well, we didn't have very good land there. One year, we had wheat, but mostly, we had rye and oats.

*For the cattle?*

Yes. And for the horses and the rest of the animals.

*Because the soil was bad?*

Well, it wasn't very good land. It wasn't heavy land.

*Mrs. Boucher, thank you very much.*

Oh, you're welcome.

*ELZEAR*
*BOUCHER,*
*known as*
*TOM BOUCHER*
*(father-in-law to*
*Agnes Boucher)*
*and*
*his second wife,*
*Eliza Peppin*

*THE YOUNG MEN OF STE. MADELEINE, 1924*
*L-R: Jean Baptiste Bercier (adopted son of Joe Bercier), Victor Bellehumeur (son of*
*Pat Bellehumeur), Louis Fleury (son of William Fleury), Felix Fleury (son of John*
*Fleury), Edward MacKay (son of Abram MacKay), Joe Venne and Joe Boucher*
*(husband of Agnes Boucher).*
*All the boys are age 17, except Louis Fleury, age 21. Taking a Sunday ride, Section*
*32, on Omar Lemay's homestead, Ste. Madeleine.*

*AGNES AND JOE BOUCHER'S*
*WEDDING DAY, 1930*
*L-R: Arthur Pritchard (Agnes'*
*uncle), Agnes, Lena Boucher*
*(Fleury) and Joe Boucher*

*JOE BOUCHER*
*as a boy,*
*at the house of his father,*
*Tom Boucher.*

*JOE BOUCHER (Agnes' husband)*
*tending cows.*

*TOM BOUCHER WITH GRANDCHILDREN*
*L-R: George, Armand, Rosalie, (Agnes' children)*
*Rose and Maria (cousins)*

## LOUIS PELLETIER

*Louis Pelletier was born December 10, 1903, in Lestock, Saskatchewan. He was the third of twelve children born to Edward Pelletier and Julie (nee) Boucher. When he was nine years old, his family moved to Ste. Madeleine where his mother's parents, Hilaire Boucher and Leocadie Perrault, homesteaded.*

*Louis had no schooling because as a young boy, he had to help his father work, scrubbing, cutting wood and threshing for farmers. Although the family's work took them away for months at a time, home was always waiting for them back in Ste. Madeleine.*

*After Louis married Pauline Fleury, they moved into their own house, but Louis continued to work summers for farmers, coming home in winter. He also worked on the crew which built the Assiniboine Bridge near St. Lazare. After the community pasture was set up, he and his family moved to Fouillard's Corner, a small resettlement area near the Gambler Indian Reserve. He continued working in the Binscarth and Foxwarren districts.*

*Louis and his wife of 45 years, had twelve children and twenty-four grandchildren. Having lost his wife a few years ago, he now lives by himself in Brandon, Manitoba, close to his brother, Harry. Eleven of his children are now living and come to visit him. At the time of this interview, he was staying in Binscarth.*

*Mr. Louis Pelletier, can I start with your age? How old are you? And when and where were you born?*

I'm 82. I was born on December 10, 1903, in Lestock, Saskatchewan.

*And who were your parents?*

Edward Pelletier and Julie Boucher.

*And did you know your grandparents on your father's side?*

It was the same name as my dad's, Edward. And Madeleine.

*What was her name before she was married?*

I can't remember that. That's so far back . . . . I used to know her maiden name but I forgot it. Maybe my brother would know.

*That's Harry? And are you all from Saskatchewan then?*

That's where I was born but I was raised here. We moved here when I was about nine years old and we stayed here ever since. I was raised right here in Manitoba.

*So that would be about 1912. Where did you move to?*

We moved to Ste. Madeleine. That's where my grandfather was—my mom's dad.

*Now, what were the names of your mother's parents?*

He was Hilaire Boucher. And, she . . . what the heck was her name? Perrault, Cadeus Perrault, something like that. She was a Perrault, I know that.

*And your great-grandparents?*

I don't remember that far back.

*Did you ever hear any stories about them?*

No, my dad and mother never told me anything about my grandparents. They never told me anything, so I don't know. Her dad and mom, that's as far back as I can remember.

*Where are your mother and father buried?*

In the cemetery across the river. In Ste. Madeleine. That's where they're all buried.

*And your great-grandparents, are they there?*

They're all there, yes.

*That's on your father's side?*

No, no. They're in Lestock, in Saskatchewan. That's where they'd been living all their lives and that's where they died. That's where they were buried, over there, see.

*How many children did your parents have?*

There were twelve of us.

*And how many are still living today?*

Well, four boys. No, three boys and four girls.

*So, there are seven of you still alive?*

Yes. There's one . . . my brother died about three months ago. Yes, not too long ago. We were four boys, right along.

*And then what about the twelve children who were born? Did they all live to be adults?*

Well, to be about twelve, thirteen, and then, they died. There were two girls who died before I was born. So they would have been older than me.

*So you were really the first child that lived. What about your own family? You got married when and to whom?*

I married Pauline Fleury. She was Frank Fleury's daughter. I couldn't say when exactly. But we had our 45th anniversary two years ago. I can't remember all those things myself. My son would remember, but I don't know how many years.

*And how many children did you have?*

We had twelve. The first one died when he was six months old. The other eleven, we saved. They're still living.

*They're all alive. And where are they now?*

They're all out on their own, here and there, all over. There are some in Saskatchewan; a daughter and son in Saskatoon, one in Regina, and two daughters in Langenburg.

*And are you a grandfather?*

Oh yes, I have twenty-four grandchildren and six great-grandchildren.

*Have you seen them all?*

I've seen them all so far, yes. I see them quite a bit. They come quite often to see me. This one from Winnipeg, he comes real often.

*What does he do in Winnipeg?*

He works construction.

*And where was he born?*

Here. In Ste. Madeleine. They were all born here.

*Who was the midwife for your twelve children? Do you remember? Or did a doctor come?*

Well, some were born in the hospital. We had three or four born at home. There was an old lady, Mrs. Bercier, she used to take care of Pauline when she had the babies. I remember she did that a long, long time ago. She died. But we had her for three or four of our kids. And for the rest, she went to the hospital. She had them in the hospital.

*Do you remember your place where you grew up in Saskatchewan?*

That town? Oh yes, I remember the town.

*Tell me about it. What was it like? How many people?*

Not too many. It was just a small, little town. A wee, small town. But now, I went through there not too long ago. I drove through there by car. I can see it's grown up a lot, that little town. I think it's bigger than this place now. Used to be two, three stores, a butcher shop and that's all. Maybe a garage. That's all there was to it. Don't believe there was even a hotel in those days. But today, they got so many places, big buildings, you know, big garages and stuff.

*When you grew up in Lestock, for those first nine years of your life, what did your father do for a living?*

He worked out on farms. He was hired labour.

*Did he make a living?*

Yes, he made a go of it. We made a living. We didn't suffer.

*Did you work with him?*

A little bit. I couldn't work too much when I was that age.

*So what did you do? Did you go to school?*

Not much school. That's how come I can't read or write. When we did move out here, I couldn't go to school. I had to help the old man make a living. We worked at one place, then on to another. We both worked so we could make a living, as best we could. Otherwise, well, we might have had a harder time, if we hadn't worked, you see. That's how come I didn't go to school. I never went to school at all. One day, I could write my name. That's all. I can't do nothing else. Can't write nothing.

*Are you unhappy about that?*

Yes, I sure am. I wish I could read and write, now. There's lots of things I'd like to read. I can't. I could learn something if I could read a little bit, but I'm just sitting here, doing nothing, just like a dummy. I can't read and you can't learn anything if you can't read. It's hard when you can't learn anything. Pretty hard. But I'm not sorry I helped dad to raise our family. I'm not sorry I helped them.

*You had no choice.*

No choice. God will forgive me for that. I hope. For helping dad. It's no sin in doing that. Nothing wrong.

*You say God will forgive you. Are you a religious man?*

Sure.

*What religion?*

Catholic. All my life. I don't know, I'm not saying I'm better than anybody else, no matter what religion. They all pray to the same God, anyway. So what's the difference? Anybody that believes in God, I guess God loves them all the same. So what's the difference?

*Mr. Pelletier, you moved in about 1912 to Ste. Madeleine, when you were nine. And you moved because your mother's father . . .*

They were living here.

*. . . were living here. Do you know when Ste. Madeleine was first established?*

I couldn't say because my grandparents were already living there quite a while. They were raised there, so I don't know how long or when Ste. Madeleine started. They were there already, those old people. My grandpa was old and those people there were old, too.

*What language did you speak in your home?*

Mostly Cree and French.

*What about English?*

English, too. We used quite a bit of English. Most of the time, when we were out working, most of the white people talked it. We could talk it as good as anybody else. That's why we talked English. My dad and mom couldn't talk English, as good. They would talk French, mostly. My grandfather could talk lots of French.

*Do you still speak Cree and French?*

Oh some. But not very much. Mostly English, now.

*Did you have much to do with the Cree people?*

No. Not too much. Oh, I can speak Cree when I have to, when I meet them, whenever I see them.

*And you learned to speak English when you were with white people.*

Well, I was out working all the time, see. Ever since I was ten, twelve years old, I'd be out working on a farm some place, all summer, all winter. I was out among white people all the time. I could talk as good as any of them.

*But when you say white people, does that mean you don't consider yourself a white person?*

No.

*What do you consider yourself?*

Metis.

*And what is a Metis?*

I don't understand what a Metis is, where it comes in. The average Metis says the same thing. What nationality it is, I don't know. There's no such thing as a Metis nationality. Metis are hybrid, I guess. I don't know what it means. That's what they call it anyways, though. We go by that.

*Are you happy to go by that name?*

I'm satisfied.

*Have you ever experienced discrimination? Have people ever made fun of you?*

Oh yes. Quite a few, yes. They make fun, but what did they get out of it? Nothing.

*What did they do?*

They laugh at you because you're black and you have a different language and you aren't the same color as them, and all that.

*You heard people say that to you? Did you fight them?*

No. Why? What do you get out of it? Nothing. You don't get anything out of it. Doesn't hurt me. Doesn't do them any good. What do they get out of it? Nothing. Just a laugh, that's all they get out of it. So, it doesn't hurt me. I don't care. If they're satisfied, good enough for me. [Laughs] It don't hurt me none. I don't care. I am what I am. Even if I were Indian or white, I'd be satisfied. Any nationality is good for me. Yes. It makes no difference.

*Now you began working with your father when you were about eleven or twelve. What kind of work?*

Well, I used to go out cutting bush and cutting wood for farmers, and all that. We used to cut a lot of wood for the farmers. I used to help. I didn't do much cutting but I used to haul that wood and pile it up for him while they were busy cutting. I'd haul it and put it in piles for them. That'd be quite a help to them.

*How much money did you get? Do you remember?*

About a dollar a load.

*And how long did it take you to make a load?*

Oh, about two or three loads a day.

*That's about two, three dollars a day. Was that good money?*

Well, in those days, the price of stuff was not very high. You bought your grub for ten dollars but you couldn't carry it home. Today, you can carry it home in a small paper bag for ten dollars. It makes a big difference. Those days, stuff was cheap. Wages weren't much, but stuff didn't cost very much, either.

*Okay, you were nine years old in 1912, and you moved to Ste. Madeleine with your parents. How many children did they have then, because you were the oldest at the time?*

I guess they must have had about three more kids after we got here. The rest we had with us.

*So there were nine of you that came from Saskatchewan. So your mother must have had a baby every year then.*

Yes, every year, just about every year. Of course, we had—I forgot to tell you—we had two sets of twins. That makes a big difference.

*Two sets of twins? And are they alive?*

No, one of each twin is alive.

*Okay. So what was Ste. Madeleine like when you got there in 1912?*

It was a nice place. Lots of bush, lots of slough, lots of hay. Good living place. People could make lots of hay for their stock in winter. Put a little crop in, nice garden and everything. Everything was nice. Lots of good wood. One of the best places there was.

*What kind of a crop?*

Well, say if you wanted to put some feed grain, like some barley or oats, or anything to feed your stock or pigs, or whatever. Put in a garden for yourself, potatoes, lots of potatoes. You could get a good crop there in the sand if you get the right kind of weather, you know. Get the wet weather, not too much, not too dry, you could raise a heck of a good crop in the sand.

*Louis, when you moved there in 1912, where did you live?*

There was a house that my grandfather had. So he let us stay in that house. He didn't use it. So we made a living in that house. We fixed it up a little bit and we moved in there and we stayed there.

*How big was the house?*

Oh, I don't know. Big enough for a living room and two bedrooms.

*No upstairs?*

Nope. Nope. Never had much upstairs in those days. All those log houses didn't have any upstairs in them, you know.

*What was the house made of?*

Logs, all logs and plaster and shingles.

*And what did you use to heat the house?*

A wood stove and a kitchen heater, both in the same house. We had lots of heat.

*Where did you get your water from?*

Nice wells. Good water in the sand when you dig a well. The best water you can get. Had lots of good water.

*And was this house close to your grandfather's house?*

About a half a mile.

*Okay now, when you moved there with your parents, brothers and sisters, did you have a deed to the place, a piece of paper? Did your father pay for the land?*

No, no, no. My grandfather had this land there, but we lived on his land. A corner of his land is where we stayed.

*How much land did your grandpa have?*

I don't know. Maybe half a section, maybe a quarter. Yes, about a quarter section, I think.

*And his name was Boucher and he had a quarter section. Did he have a paper, a deed, a title?*

Oh well, you had to have it.

*Did you ever see it?*

No, not me. Not too crazy about a thing like that, no. You have to have a deed. You have to have a paper to pay your tax every year, huh? You had to have your paper.

*Did your grandfather pay his taxes?*

Oh yes.

*Every year?*

Until he died, yes.

*When did he die?*

Oh, I couldn't say when but quite a while ago.

*Did he die after Ste. Madeleine was disbanded or before?*

Before. Before they ever started the pasture, he died.

*So when he died, who took over his land?*

Joe Boucher's dad.

*Who's dad?*

Joe Boucher's dad took over the place.

*I don't understand.*

JOE BOUCHER'S DAD!

*Oh. Joe Boucher's dad took over.*

Took over the place. Yes.

*Oh, I see. And were you still allowed to live on the land?*

Well, we weren't there anymore. We moved some place else. We didn't stay there steady, you know. We'd be out some place, working for somebody out in the country. We'd go live there, where the farmers were. They'd give us a place to live. We'd live there and work right there. But after the work, we'd always come home.

*So you moved to Ste. Madeleine with your family in 1912, and you lived about half a mile from your grandfather, but not permanently?*

Not steady. We'd go home, now and then. We still had the house there but we'd be out working most of the time, then back home, once in a while. Back and forth, you see. We didn't leave the house for good. We still had the house to go home to whenever we could.

*So this was like home to you?*

Yes. It was our home. That's what we depend on to go to, whenever we wanted to go back home.

*I see. And did you do this right up until there was no Ste. Madeleine? Or did you stop going back there, after a while?*

Well, after I got married, I still had the house there, but I used to go out working. I used to leave my house all summer, like I did when I was young. Come back and forth to my house for the winter. Spring, I'd have to go away to work all summer and go back home again in the fall.

*When did you leave Ste. Madeleine and never go back again?*

That was when they built that pasture. They told us to get out. We had to get out.

*Who were they?*

The fellow that ran the community pasture from Lazare.

*Who was that?*

John Selby, they called him. He was the head man there, so they told us to get out.

*What did he tell you?*

They told us they'd give us a house, a place to live, same kind we had if we moved out. Wherever we wanted to be. And give us so much money to start us up wherever we lived. So they moved some people to Selby Town. He built houses for them, all right. He built a few houses, three or four there, but these ones here on top of the hill here, where the church is, he never built anything there. They'd be able to build their own houses there.

*You say on top of the hill. Do you mean Fouillard's Corner?*

Fouillard's Corner, that's what they used to call it. And the other one's Selby Town. Selby built houses but Fouillard didn't build any. Selby's doing all this on his own, you see.

*Did you get any money? Did they promise you money?*

Some money, $25.

*You got $25? Because Joe Venne got $150.*

Well, some of them got more than that, too.

*How come you only got $25?*

I don't know. I had a family. They didn't give me no more than $25 and I had no place to go. When I got here, where am I suppose to go? We parked a tent and stayed in there for the summer until I could make some kind of a house to stay in.

*So you stayed in a tent in Selby Town?*

Stayed in a tent all summer in Fouillard. That's where I parked. I didn't want to go settle down anywhere else. I wanted to stay here.

*So you were at the Corner. And did you build a house there?*

Yes, I finally built a little house, so I had a cover over my kitchen.

*And how long did you stay there?*

All my life.

*In Fouillard's Corner? This was after you were kicked out of the pasture, out of Ste. Madeleine?*

Yes. That's where we had to stay. I finally got a house, maybe ten, twelve years later. On account of I was on welfare. Maybe it was less than that. See, I was sick. I was trying to work but I was so sick, I couldn't do anything. I couldn't eat. One day, there was a health nurse going around checking the people. She came to my place. I was standing in the doorway.

She says, "Stop everything. You're sick."

I said, "I know I'm sick. But what can I do?"

She said, "Well, what do you do for it?"

I said, "Well, I go to work a little bit. Try to make a living."

"You can't work. How are you going to make a living when you're sick like that? You're going to have to see the doctor," she said.

I said, "I got no money. Don't want to see the doctor."

"You'll go. I'll give you a paper. A paper from me. You'll go to see the doctor."

I went to Russell and gave the doctor the paper.

*You went to Russell?*

Yes. I didn't know it but she wanted the doctor to sign the form to get me the welfare. She takes me up to the doctor, fills out the forms. "You mail this," she said.

I mailed this paper and in about two weeks, I received a cheque from welfare. Since then I've been having help, you see. All the time, I've been sick, I couldn't work for about five years. I wasn't working at all. So I got help from welfare.

One day, a social worker came and I asked, "Can I get a house built, better than what I got?" I had an old log house there. "If I get some new logs," I said, "and fix my house, could you give me the lumber to finish it, and roofing and the flooring and the windows and doors?"

*This is in Fouillard's Corner?*

This is in Fouillard, yes.

This welfare guy said, "Ah, logs are no good; I think you'd be better to build a frame house. It'd be cheaper and faster. You'll have a cleaner house. Less work. We'll give you some lumber. You build a frame house."

They gave me lumber. I built a frame house at the Corner. I had Hydro and everything. After I got better, I started working out on farms all over. My family had a good home there. Wood house. It had Hydro, everything; a machine to wash clothes. My wife didn't have to wash with her board anymore. [Laughs] She had a machine to wash with. Had other things, too. Everything! So I was all right. I was working out with farmers.

*I read that the reason people were told to leave Ste. Madeleine was because of the PFRA. Did you know about it?*

Yes.

*They told you about it? What did you think about it, at the time, because you were in your 30s then?*

Yes, well, there was nothing much I could do about it, whatever I thought. I just had to go their way, I guess, whatever they wanted. There was a fellow there, went to Lazare. He had a piece of land, too. Not big, I guess. But he went over there with his money to pay his tax and somebody refused him. Wouldn't take his money. Told him, "It's no use for you to pay the taxes. You don't own the place anymore. Turned it into pasture now."

*So who was the man?*

It was Vermette. He went to pay his tax. And this Selby said, "No, you can't pay your taxes. It's all one piece now. It's all a big pasture. What good is it, you alone on that small, little piece of land? There's no use for you to pay for that land. It's not yours anymore. It's all going to be pasture. You might as well save your money."
   So, he came home. He didn't pay his tax. He lost his land and everything.

*Did he get another piece of land to replace the land he lost?*

No. He was parked here, too.

*The federal government told all Canadians, not just Metis people, that when agricultural land was made into pastureland, they would give you an equivalent amount of acreage, if you had paid your tax. Agnes Boucher said they got the land they now have because it was land the government promised them. If you didn't pay your taxes, you were a squatter and they didn't give you anything.*

Yes, I know that. Tax got to be paid. Oh yes. But I never had nothing to pay taxes for. I was a squatter there, same as everybody else. There was a whole lot of them living there. Maybe we were living on somebody else's land. Nobody seemed to mind. I guess the taxes didn't amount to very much because there was a lot of unbroken land there, see. It was mostly all prairie. Not much cultivated land.

*Did you consider that Metis land?*

Oh yes, we did but what could we do? We couldn't hang on to it after they got these things going. All the papers were fixed up; signed up to get that pasture going. That's all there was to it. There were a lot of people who lived there when they were building that pasture. And some of the people worked to help build that pasture.

*Metis people?*

Yes. The people who lived there and helped build the pasture. But after, they had to get out because they finished the pasture.

*What do you think of it now, 48 years later?*

I let it be forgot a long time ago. It's so long ago, I think it's gone. No more memory about it. I doubt that anyone thinks about that anymore. It would be a good thing in a way, for the young generation to have something of their own, to live and all that. But nowadays, I don't know, young people would sooner be out in some big city, some place where they can make some good money, working some big job, you know.

*In Winnipeg?*

Yes, in big jobs like that. Make good money. They don't want to go out in the country and start farming or raising cattle. I don't think young people would want to do it anymore.

*So Louis, are you saying when the Metis people were told to leave in 1938, that it was a good thing?*

In those days, they might have made something out of it then, because they were starting to do something. They had cultivated the land; it was broken. Quite a few people had cattle and horses, chickens, pigs and everything. They had put in crops, wheat, barley, oats, everything. They might have made a go of it in those days. But now . . . I don't think anybody would start that stuff. They want to do construction, nowadays—big money.

*But were you sorry to leave in 1939?*

Well, I was because I had no place to go. No home. Burned my house down. Where am I going to stay? No place to go.

*They burned your house down?*

They burned them all down.

*Did you see it?*

Well, it was all ashes.

*Who burned it?*

I don't know who, but somebody must have. Every house was down after everybody moved out. Of course, there was nothing in them. Houses were no good, I guess. They might as well be burned. But we were supposed to get the same kind of house we left there behind.

*And you never did?*

We got nothing.

*You had to build it on your own?*

All I got was $25. Some got $100; some got maybe $200 or $300. I don't know. Some probably got quite a bit. They moved some people from here to Camperville. It cost quite a bit to move them there but they paid for it.

*To Camperville. That's in Saskatchewan?*

No. Camperville is Manitoba. Yes. Duck Bay and all that over there. Northeast, I guess, from Dauphin. Some place out there, that's Camperville. Where the lakes are.

*Did your life change after you moved out of Ste. Madeleine?*

Didn't make much difference. Just kept on living the same old way. Working. Made a living for my family. That's all I worried about. I didn't care about anything else.

*But the community wasn't there anymore. Did you miss that?*

Oh, I missed part of it but that didn't keep me from working, anyways. As long as I was getting some work to make a living for my kids, I didn't care. Company came and went. I didn't care about my company because they weren't helping me make a living, anyways. [Laughs] Ah, it's no good. That's all we got out of it. We haven't had a home since. The only time was when I had that new house built; only time I had a home, after the pasture.

*When was that new home built for you?*

I don't exactly know. It's about roughly eighteen, nineteen years ago, but I sold it. Mrs. Boucher's son bought the house. I guess he must have hauled it home to his place.

*Back to 1939, when you think of John Selby, was he a good man? How did he treat you?*

He was a good man in one way. He used to help the people quite a bit, you know. When the people were out of work, he'd give them a handout once in a while, give them relief. Give them some groceries, give them an order in the store. Keep them going, so they wouldn't go hungry. He was good like that in one way. Good-hearted. But this thing, I don't know. I guess it was money for him to get that pasture going. I guess that's why he turned. He took that job. Didn't care what happened to us. I guess it was his job to give some money or something to build places for them. But he didn't do it for all of us, just for some. Those living in the valley there, he built houses for them. I don't know how much money he gave them but I know some of them got quite a bit of money.

I always think I lived through it all. Everything. After, all my kids grew up; they went on and it was all right. I didn't have any worries. I just had my old lady with me. Now without my old lady, I'm worse now. [Sighs] All by myself. And sick all the time.

*If I could go back to Ste. Madelaine, when you were there with your family, what kind of meals did your wife prepare?*

Everything. All kinds of stuff. She used to cook some vegetables, have some chicken.

*Prairie chicken?*

Prairie chicken, yes. And jumper meat. Canned jumper. Jumpers were good when they were canned. Used to can that kind of stuff and keep it in jars, pickle jars. Now and then, we warmed it up. Wow! It's good stuff. We had lots of potatoes, canned vegetables, carrots, everything. Big gardens. Oh, we were never hungry. We had a lot of food, lots of jumpers, lots of chickens, lots of partridge, too. We used partridge and ducks.

*You got them in Ste. Madeleine, in the bush?*

Oh yes, down by the river, you can get all you want.

*Which river?*

Down by the Assiniboine River. Lots of sloughs there, too. Lots of meat there, all over, no matter where you went.

*Who were some of your best friends in Ste. Madeleine?*

Most of them were my best friends. [Laughs] No enemies I had—not many enemies. They were all good friends. They were all good people then. In those days, the people couldn't have been any better; they were all good. Help one another; do anything for anybody. Give them a chance to help you, they helped you. Oh yes, people were good in those days.

*How did they help you, for example?*

If you needed to get something done and you were behind time or something, in our days they'd come and give you a hand. Get it done in no time. Yes.

*Louis, when you think of Ste. Madeleine, what were some of the good times there? Did you have good times there?*

I had lots of good times, lots of good people, lots of parties, everything. Never had any trouble of any kind. Not like they have nowadays. They have lots of trouble all the time. Nobody has a good time anymore. They don't know what a good time is anymore. Not like those days. We knew what a good time was.

*What was a party like? Did you have alcohol?*

A good party? Oh, we had some drinking parties and dances and everything. We used to have some really good times. Everybody could play guitar, violin.

*Did you have booze at the parties? In those days?*

We used to have a little bit, not too much. Never used to get overloaded. Not like they do today. There's always been booze, as far as that goes. Whatever kind of parties they had, they knew how to handle their booze. They didn't make pigs out of themselves. They used to know how much to drink; knew how to control their booze, control themselves. I never was a drunkard. I haven't drank for five, six years, I guess. I haven't drank for a long, long time. I quit drinking. Since my old lady started getting sick, I quit. It didn't help, didn't help at all. I lost her anyways.

*Back to Ste. Madeleine, do you think the government should help those people who were moved off the land? Do you think they should get something, those few people who are left, or their children?*

Well, I'm sure a few would be glad to go back, if they knew they could get help to start up. But to go on their own, they'd never make a go now. Like I said, nowadays, young people want the big cities, making big money, construction jobs, all kinds of work, making big money, ten, twelve, eighteen dollars an hour. That's what they're looking for now. And they wouldn't make that over there.

*How much money did you make back then?*

The last time I worked out on farms all over up until when I couldn't work anymore, I used to work for $30 a week; $30 in a whole week was what I used to make. I used to come home here to the Corner on Saturdays. Sunday night, back to work again over there for another week, for $30 a week. That's what my wages were.

*Louis, let me ask you one final question: how do you want people to remember you? What do you want them to think about you?*

I don't know. Think about me as what I am, I guess. That's all. I've got no enemies. I've got lots of friends, all over the world, no matter where I go. All my friends, everybody, even these people in town here, they all like me. I'm good to them. They're good to me. You'll never see me stuck. When you're loved by everybody, that way, that's good. If you're no good, then nobody likes you. That's the way I look at it.

*Well, Louis, thank you very much.*

Yes, okay.

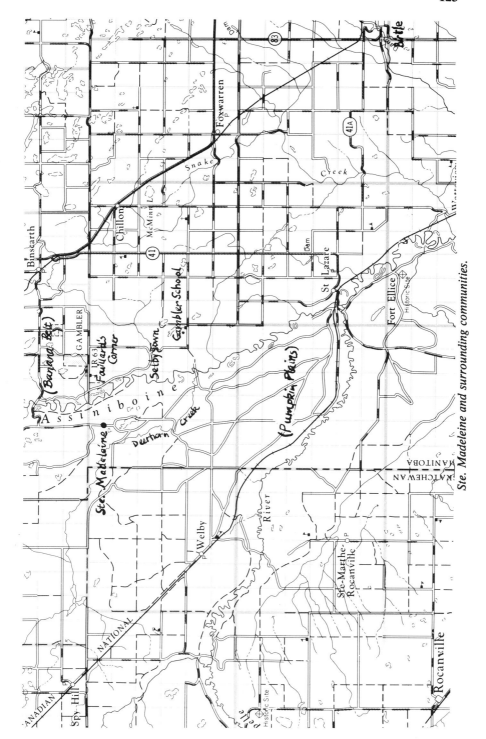

*Ste. Madeleine and surrounding communities.*

Map grid with the following sections:

- **31** RAILWAY 1882
- **32** Joseph Omar Lemay 1908 / Pascal Alfred Lemay 1907 ✳ ✝ ✳
- **33** RAILWAY 1902
- **34** GAMBLER / INDIAN RESERVE
- **30** William Larose 1915 / Alex Flammund 1914 / Roger Ducharme 1917
- **29** DEER HORN CREEK / BELLIVEAU SCHOOL 1921
- **28** Alexandre Vermette 1908 / Louis Boucher 1906 / Louis Fleury 1910 / Wilfred Vermette 1907
- **27** RAILWAY 1883
- **19** RAILWAY 1882
- **20** William Fleury 1920 / Gregoirie Ledoux 1908
- **21** RAILWAY 1882
- **22** UNIV. OF MANITOBA 1898 / Isadore Fleury 1921 / ASSINIBOINE RIVER
- **18** Alexander Smith 1918 / Paul Ducharme 1916 / Claphase Ducharme 1917
- **17** RAILWAY 1882
- **16** Nelson Boyd 1913 / Clodia Fleury 1922 / Marie Bellehumeur 1910 / Guillaume LeFranc 1910
- **15** Sara Caroline Bitner 1922
- **7** RAILWAY 1882
- **8** HUDSON'S BAY COMPANY 1881
- **9** RAILWAY 1882
- Baptiste Fleury 1918 / Francois Demerais 1893 / Ambroise Fisher 1920 / Leo Favreau 1905

✳ Ambroise Ledoux 1911

⌂ Ste. Madeleine Church, built in 1913.

*ORIGINAL STE. MADELEINE HOMESTEADS, TOWNSHIP 18, RANGE 29*
*These 20 sections (of a total of 36 in the Township) included the majority of the Ste. Madeleine residents. The even-numbered sections were set aside for homesteads. Over the years, the land changed hands among family and community members. The dates (from the Township General Register, Department of Interior) below the names indicate when the land patent was granted.*
*Hilaire Boucher, grandfather to Agnes' husband, Lena Fleury and Louis and Harry Pelletier, lived on Section 28, close to his brother, Louis Boucher. Joe Venne's grandfather, Baptiste Fleury, homesteaded on Section 10.*

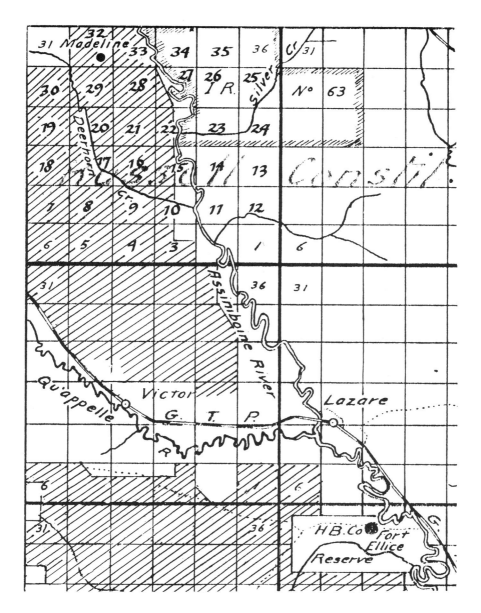

THE COMMUNITY PASTURE

*Captain John Palliser, in his 1857 survey for the British government, identified 20 million hectares of prairie land which was too dry to support farming. Nevertheless, in 1872, this area was opened up for homesteading. To deal with the serious problem of drought in the 1930s, the PFRA set up community pastures across the prairies. [Diagonal lines indicate the boundaries of the pastureland in the Ste. Madeleine area, Ellice Municipality.]*

## HARRY PELLETIER

*Harry Pelletier, Louis Pelletier's younger brother, was born in Indian Head, Saskatchewan, on July 4, 1905. His parents, Edward Pelletier and Julie Boucher, homesteaded in Jasmin, Saskatchewan, later moving to Lestock, close to the Muskowekwan Indian Reserve. The family, with six children at the time, then moved to Ste. Madeleine, where Julie's father, Hilaire Boucher, homesteaded.*

*At twenty, Harry began to work for the CNR, which took him to Saskatchewan. In 1930, Harry became a representative of a newly-founded association of Saskatchewan Metis. He travelled in that province, speaking and organizing to reclaim land rights. When he returned to Ste. Madeleine in 1938, he was sad to find that the community had been disbanded.*

*When World War II broke out, Harry joined the army where he stayed until 1946. In 1943, he had married Lena (nee Fleury) and they had two children before the wartime forced their separation in 1946. In 1948, Harry had a common-law marriage with Alice Spence and they had three children. This marriage lasted until Alice died in 1978.*

*Harry is actively involved with the Manitoba Metis Federation [MMF] struggle to reclaim Metis land rights. He lives in Brandon with his son, George, also an active MMF member. Harry continues to be an inspiration to young Metis people in the southwest region.*

*Harry, what did you have for lunch today?*

Oh, I had some macaroni and meat and butter and jam, milk and tea. I don't use sugar. I'm not supposed to use . . . .

*Diabetes?*

Yes.

*Did you make it yourself . . .*

Oh yes.

*. . . or did George make it?*

No, I cooked it myself.

*Okay, Harry, would you tell me when and where you were born?*

July 4, 1905, in Indian Head, Saskatchewan.

*How many children were there in the family?*

There were eight girls and four boys. I didn't see the first two girls. They died before I was born.

*So how many of the children are still alive?*

There's three girls and three boys.

*And you're 81 years old?*

I'll be 81 on the fourth of July.

*And how do you feel? Are you in good shape?*

No. I get heart attacks sometimes. Then I had an operation for my food passage. My gallstone was taken out. Then I had a stroke six, seven years ago.

*But you still get around?*

Yes.

*And how come you're here in Brandon?*

To be close to the doctor and the hospital, you know. And so George will be able to get around for the MMF. He's working at the bingos, lots of times, selling tickets or something.

*And what about your wife?*

She's down in Binscarth.

*She is. I see. And when were you married?*

In March 1943.

*So you were 38 when you got married?*

Oh yes.

*You waited a long time. You playing hard to get?*

Well, I was in the army, eh.

*The Canadian Army. When did you join?*

In 1939.

*Where did you go?*

Jamaica.

*Jamaica. That sounds like a holiday.*

Yeah, Jamaica. We didn't stay there very long. We came back to Winnipeg, then stayed in Shilo until the war was over.

*So you didn't see any action?*

No, no. Just lots of planes flying around.

*How many children did you have?*

Well, I had two with my first wife, Lena. She's in Binscarth now. The boy was born first, then the girl.

*You had two marriages?*

Well, I had one common-law marriage with Alice Spence—she's George's mother.

*How many children did you have with your common-law wife?*

Three.

*So, you married in 1943. And when did you live with your common-law wife?*

In 1948.

*You had three with George's mother, Alice Spence, and two with your first wife, Lena. So where is your common-law wife?*

Oh, she died about seven, eight years ago. We lived together quite a few years. Our first one was a girl but she died. And the next one was George. And another one, a boy, died in birth. We lost two. I've just got George.

*So, in all, you had five children. How many are living now?*

Well, there's only George and Margaret.

*Margaret is George's sister?*

No, half-sister.

*Right. I see. So tell me the names of your mother and father.*

Edward Pelletier and Julie Boucher.

*Oh, she was a Boucher. The famous Boucher family. They're all over. And now your mother's family. Her parents?*

Hilaire Boucher and his wife was Cadeus Perrault.

*Did you meet them? Did you know them?*

I saw them when I was a little kid. I still remember them.

*And on your father's side? Your grandparents' names?*

Edward Pelletier and Madeleine Morin.

*And can you go back a generation more? Who were your great-grandparents on your father's side?*

My great-grandfather was a Pelletier. I don't know his name, though. I forget. It's a long way back. His wife was an Indian woman. A Blackfoot Indian.

*You know that much. And then, on your mother's side?*

I don't remember. Their names were Boucher. They were . . . not Belgian. I guess they were half German and half French.

*You were born in Indian Head, Saskatchewan in 1905. When did you get to Ste. Madeleine?*

Well, in 1914, 1915, after the First World War broke out. The following summer.

*You were about nine, ten years old?*

Yes, about that.

*Did you go to school? Did you have any schooling?*

Well, I didn't go to school in Saskatchewan, only in Ste. Madeleine.

*How long did you go?*

Well, I went to school in the winter only. Summer, I had to go out working. My dad was working, cutting scrub or something like that, cutting wood. We had to help him make hay. We had to work with him. Then in winter, we'd go to school. We used to go to school in that old church there.

*Oh, in the church. Not in Belliveau School?*

Belliveau School was built later.

*Oh, I see.*

I went there for about one year, I think. Then I was out of school.

*So how many years of schooling did you have all together?*

Oh, I don't know. Maybe three or four years.

*Can you read and write?*

Oh, I can read a little bit, yeah.

*English and French?*

No. Just English.

*And what language did you speak in your father's house?*

French.

*What about Indian languages?*

Well, I learned Indian languages later. Cree and Saulteaux.

*Cree and Saulteaux. And do you still know them now?*

Oh yes.

*How did you learn them?*

Just chumming around with those boys and girls, the kids playing around. I learned from there. Because my dad was in the treaty before.

*You mean he was a treaty Indian?*

Yes. Well, he wasn't Indian but he was treaty. When the scrips came down at Fort Qu'Appelle, the land scrips and money scrips, they gave us some land.

*It came from Ottawa?*

No. The Queen Victoria.

*Oh, it came from England. And this was what year?*

Oh good God, I don't know. Cause they were just married and my dad took his land scrip. And my mother took a land scrip. That's 240 acres of scrip.

*Together?*

For one. It was 480 acres together. And my dad sold his for $50, which was robbing the poor people, eh. So after my dad sold his, he took a homestead in Jasmin, Saskatchewan. I don't know where he had his scrips because I wasn't born yet. But they talked about it lots of times.

*Your mother and father. And they were mad?*

Yeah. Well, they were mad because they sold it. I don't know why they sold it. I guess they were hard up or something.

*And when your father sold his scrips, he was no longer considered treaty?*

No. He came out of treaty before he took the scrips.

*Then he was considered . . . .*

An outsider. But he was still . . . what do you call it? Years ago, they used to call it half-breeds. Call it Metis. Metis is the French language. They call it Metis today. I don't even understand what Metis means myself. Just a sort of hybrid, half Indian and half French.

*But in fact, you only had one Indian grandmother who was a Blackfoot. There's only one Indian ancestor in your background?*

Yes. Oh yes, but my grandparents were Metis.

*Can you tell me what the word Metis means to you?*

Well, you see, the Indians belong to this country. This is their land. Then these French people came here, and also the Scotch, the Irish and the English. And they didn't bring any women with them. So they got married to the Indian women. That's where the Metis come from. They married these Indian women so they can have kids who speak their language. So they can translate the language to one another. See, when these kids were born, they were hybrids. Their fathers are French or Scotch or English, and their mothers were Indian. So then they can talk both languages, their mothers' and their fathers'. So that's how they used their kids, eh.

*So, your father had a homestead in Saskatchewan. Where was the homestead? Do you remember it?*

Jasmin. I remember that place real good, yeah.

*How many acres was it?*

It was 165 acres.

*And what did he have on that land?*

Well, he had horses, cattle and chickens. He grew some wheat, a garden, and stuff like that. He had everything.

*Was he a good manager? Hard worker?*

Oh yes. He was trapping at the same time, in winter and spring.

*Your father was a good farmer in Saskatchewan. So why did he go to Ste. Madeleine, if he was doing . . . .*

I don't know. I don't know. After he sold his homestead, we had no place to live.

*He sold his homestead. Were you around then?*

Yes, I was around. But I don't remember. I was a little kid.

*You were a kid then. How old were you when he sold it?*

Oh gosh, I don't know. I don't remember that.

*And was he sad after he sold it?*

Well, I guess so. After he realized he made a mistake.

*Did he have to sell it? Did your father drink? Was he drunk when it happened? Or something like that?*

I don't know. He was drinking, all right. But I don't know if he was drinking at the time he sold that land, eh.

*Tell me what the homestead in Jasmin looked like.*

I remember that place just like I see it today. It was all prairies, bushes and lakes. There was a lake right behind the house, a deep lake. It wasn't big but it was deep. The house was on the south side of the lake.

*What kind of house?*

A log house.

*How big was it?*

I don't know. Just one room. In those days, they didn't have bedrooms, kitchens and living rooms. They just had one room. The beds were right there, everything. We were living in that room.

*You slept in the same room as your mother and father?*

Yeah. Oh yeah.

*They didn't have any privacy? Did they have a curtain or something around their bed?*

No. No, I don't think so. I don't remember that. But there was a barn on the west side of the house. A log barn. And a sod roof.

*A sod roof? You mean the logs were cut in half?*

Yes. But then they were covered up with sod instead of shingles. Sod is good. It was a warm building. There was no frost going through there.

*And what did you have in that barn?*

Well, they had horses, cattle and . . . .

*And you milked cows and had butter and cream and that?*

Oh yes. My mother used to milk the cows. My dad never milked the cows. My mother, she was good at that. Old Boucher always had lots of cattle . . . . So then they moved to Lestock, Saskatchewan, close to the Muskowekwan Reserve. Close to the Red River cart road, the Old Telegraph Trail they called it. We lived there for quite a few years. And the war broke out.

*When I spoke to your brother, Louis, who is two years older than you, he said he was born in Lestock, Saskatchewan. So was he born there and then you moved to Indian Head?*

Could be. They were travelling, you know.

*So your father had this homestead in Jasmin, for eight, nine years?*

I guess so. Because I remember when Christmas came, he used to come in there. They put us to bed, then put the Christmas presents out. I remember because I was playing on a lumber floor. I got a sliver here on my right thumb, eh, on the floor, pushing toys. That's why I remember so good. [Laughs]

*What kind of presents did you get?*

It was mostly wood and stuff like that. In those days, it wasn't very classy. The girls had toy dolls.

*Okay, the war broke out in 1914, and in about 1915, you went over to Ste. Madeleine. Why did you go there? Did you know anybody?*

Well, my mother's relations were there.

*The Bouchers. So, she knew the people there?*

Yes.

*Do you remember the day you moved to Ste. Madeleine?*

Well, it was summer anyways. We got off the train in St. Lazare. Some guys from St. Lazare took us down to my grandfather's home, old Boucher's place. Then from there they gave us a house.

*Your grandfather had an empty house?*

Yes, there was a house there. My uncle used to live there, eh. Jacques Boucher, they called him. He died long ago. But there was no floor. There were windows but no floor. And the roof was covered with sod. That's what I remember.

*And no furniture?*

Yes, we had furniture. They gave us furniture.

*You got to this place in 1915, and you were all busy getting the place fixed up. Did your father put plank flooring down after a while?*

Well yes, but we stayed there all winter, without a floor.

*And what about water?*

There was a well there.

*Were the neighbours close by?*

Only my grandfather. He was about a quarter mile from there.

*And this land that he gave you, did it have land where you could do farming? Where you could have animals?*

No. That land belonged to my grandfather.

*You were visitors. Did your grandfather ever say you could have it for six months, a year?*

No. There was no limit.

*Did he charge you money for staying there?*

Oh no. No.

*It was free. Your father sold his homestead, so did he have any money when he arrived in Ste. Madeleine?*

I guess he must have had a little. We stayed there. Then we moved to a different place. It was a big house.

*In Ste. Madeleine?*

Yes. With an upstairs. The Ducharmes were living there. They moved out to St. Ambroise, north of Portage. I don't know how many years we stayed there. That's the time my grandfather's brother died. Louis Boucher.

*So how long did you stay in Ste. Madeleine?*

Well, I was raised there. In the winter, we stayed there but in summer, we'd go out, cutting scrub. My dad worked on the farms.

*So your mother and father and all the kids went, too?*

Yes. We used to live in a big tent. I remember that. [Laughs] We had a stove. We made a good living.

*But you all had to work?*

We all had to work, all that we could.

*It was tough times. You really didn't have a childhood. You were born and you became a man.*

Yes. Then my mother died. I don't know what year she died. It was 1925 or 1926. My mother died about that time.

*So you were about 20. What did she die from?*

Appendix. She took sick in the morning and died the next morning.

*No doctor?*

No doctor. Tried Dr. Gilbart in Spy Hill. But he didn't have a chance to get there.

*And what about the people who lived in the community? Were there no people who had folk medicine?*

We didn't know anything about appendix, in those days. In Binscarth, there was Dr. Lanigan but we didn't have a chance to go and get him. There were no cars at that time. There were just cutters.

*What about your dad, was he a good man?*

Oh yes. He was good-natured.

*He gave you what you needed. Did he ever beat you?*

Oh yeah! Course, we kids had to be straightened up, so he gave us quite a few lickings. But we deserved it. We were awful. I remember Louis and me, we were awful, teasing the girls, eh. Teasing the other kids, fighting with the other kids. He had to straighten us up. He sure did. My mother did, too. But they were good people. Strong religion. Very, very strong religion.

*Which religion?*

Roman Catholic.

*And did you keep to that religion, too?*

Oh yeah, I kept my religion right up to now.

*Now, can you tell me how big Ste. Madeleine was? How many sections of land would it have covered?*

Well, let's see now . . . five miles square, anyways. It must have been pretty near a township. From the boundary of Saskatchewan down to the river. That's quite a ways.

*While you lived in Ste. Madeleine, at your grandfather Boucher's place, did you ever pay taxes?*

No, no.

*If you paid no money, no rent, you had no land entitlement while you were there. So in a sense, you were squatters.*

Well, my dad used to rent that crown land, eh, for pasture for the cattle and the horses, in St. Lazare, there. It's crown land, see. He paid five cents an acre.

*He would rent it from the government, in the summertime?*

Yes. He was making hay. We used to get fifteen cents a ton for making hay on crown land.

*Was that good money?*

Oh yes. We used to cut hay there and . . . .

*When you say we, who are you talking about?*

My dad and my brother, Louis.

*The three of you. That's all?*

Well, my mother and my sisters, they all helped.

*Your mother and your sisters. So you worked as a family?*

Oh yes.

*And even when you were grown up, when you were 25, 30, you still worked together as a family?*

Oh yes.

*Okay, now let me see if I have this straight. In 1915, you moved to St. Madeleine to your grandfather's house. Then you moved to the Ducharme house. And in the summertime, you would live in a tent and go scrubbing. But your family's home was always in Ste. Madeleine?*

Yes.

*And where was the barn where you kept the cattle?*

Well, we didn't have cattle there at the Ducharme house. Later, we had a house down in the valley close to the river.

*So you had a third house. And did your father build the house? Did you help him build it?*

No, he got it from somebody else. The house was built already. But my dad built the barn.

*What year was this approximately?*

Well, I think we lived there two, three years, when my mother died. That's where she died.

*And your mother died about 1925, so you moved there about 1923, around there?*

Yes.

*And after she died, did you continue to live there?*

After she died, in the same year, my dad moved back to Lestock, Saskatchewan, again.

*And he took you with him?*

No, I had cattle and horses. Then my sister, Emma—the oldest, she was fourteen, fifteen—went to Crane River with my uncle. So I gave her four head of cattle to take along.

*Why did she go with your uncle?*

I don't know. She was a grown-up girl anyways. So I gave her the four head of cattle to go along with her. I don't know what she did with them. I gave them to her anyhow. Then I had horses and sold them to a woman from St. Joseph.

*Why did you sell them?*

Well, I had no use for them. I was alone, eh.

*Where was Louis?*

He was out working. He was a man. I don't know where. He worked for the Newmans or something like that, north of Binscarth. He worked there quite a few years. Anyways, I took off. I went to Saskatchewan after I sold everything.

*How long did you stay by yourself?*

Oh, not very long. About a year, I guess. Then I started working on the railroad, on one of those gangs. CNR. That's what they called the Grand Trunk in those days. I was a water boy. I started hauling water for the men. It was a pump car. And in about two years, I started working in the section.

*You never went back to Ste. Madeleine?*

Not that time. After that, I finished in Welby.

*Did you get paid well?*

Oh yes. It was good money, 30 cents an hour. Then I went to work at Weldon, Saskatchewan and . . . .

*What did you do there?*

Worked in a section.

*Oh, I see. Farm help.*

No. In a section.

*Oh. A section gang for the railroad?*

Yes. Then I went to Lestock and I worked there for two years in railroads. Then I got a yard job in Melville. The road master transferred me to the yard engine room, and I started cooling off engines. Then they put me on the weigh freight.

*What did you do?*

Firing.

*Oh really? You were a fireman, then?*

Yes.

*Did you like that?*

Yes. Oh yes.

*How many years did you do that?*

Two years.

*And during the time you were doing all this kind of work, you stayed away from Ste. Madeleine? You didn't see your father or your sisters or your brother?*

I saw some of my sisters. Then I quit the railroad. I think it was 1930. That's the time the MMF started.

*The MMF? The Manitoba Metis Federation?*

Well, it was a Saskatchewan Metis federation. Then I was doing good. They sent me down to Lebret. I stayed there, talking to people. Then the president came there.

*Who was the president?*

John Ross. They've got that reserve there at Frog Lake, which is sixty miles long and six miles wide. It belongs to the Metis people.

*Given to them by the Saskatchewan or the Ottawa government?*

Both.

*Did they give you money for working for them?*

Well, they paid my travelling expenses and my board, where I camped and everything.

*Why did you do this work for the Metis federation? Did you feel strongly for the Metis people?*

Well, yes. I believed in them. Because in Saskatchewan, we stuck together, eh. We all stuck together, just like the fingers on one hand.

*Why?*

For the rights. The Metis rights and the land claim rights. So, we got the land all right. But I didn't get in.

*Do they still have that land?*

Yes. Oh yes. They've got houses, a hospital and drugstores. They've got stores and everything. They're doing good, very good.

*But you say you didn't get in. What does that mean?*

The land claim. See, I was in the paper there. Ross wanted me to travel. I was all alone and I was young. I was travelling so I lost my chance. See, I came down to Ste. Madeleine. I tried to gather a lot of Metis there, to claim Ste. Madeleine as a reserve. Not a treaty. Just a land claim. To get funded by the government. But they didn't want to sign it. Only four signed.

*Why didn't they want to sign it?*

They didn't want to be treaty, like Indians.

*Who were the four?*

Old Paul Ducharme, Johnny Fleury, Fred Boyer and old August Vermette.

*What about Joe Venne?*

Joe Venne wasn't around then. Joe was south someplace close to the boundary.

*So you went there and you wanted to get the government in Ottawa to make Ste. Madeleine into a reserve?*

Yes, and to get some of these people to start a Metis federation, like in Saskatchewan. I don't know. It seemed to me Manitoba was always behind. So I went back to Lebret and we had a meeting there.

*Who had the meeting?*

John Ross. And there was an Indian helping the Metis. He was Saulteaux from, what they call, Duck Lake in Saskatchewan.

*And you worked with them?*

Sure, but I lost track of them after I came down to Ste. Madeleine here. But after I went back to Lebret, we had a meeting there. We were talking about Ste. Madeleine. And he says, "Forget about them. It's no use. They're bucking us. Leave them alone. They'll get to realizing someday."

*What year did you go to Ste. Madeleine to try to get the Metis people to form a reserve?*

I tried in 1932. Then I went back to Saskatchewan. I didn't come back until oh, about 1938, 1939.

*Why did you come back?*

I just came for a visit. See how the people were making out.

*And what did you find?*

There was nobody there. A few people still, but that's all. I don't know if that's the year the pasture came. The time I came back, they'd moved their houses, their furniture . . . .

*Who were they?*

You called them John Selby and Fouillard. So that's what I heard. I don't know for sure, but I know John Selby was a municipal officer and he was the one that come down and told them to get out. They were going to make a pasture and put cattle in there.

*You were there in 1938? What season?*

It was in summer.

*And there weren't very many people there?*

Oh, no. No.

*But there were some still?*

Some.

*Agnes and Joe were still there?*

They were down in the valley. They were all scattered all over. I went to what they called Selby Town, down in the Silver Creek area, and to Fouillard's Corner, beside the reserve there, over at Binscarth. I found the people scattered all over. I didn't realize what was going on. They were building the fence, I guess.

*Did you talk to the people who were moved?*

Yes.

*What was their spirit like?*

Well, they didn't seem to mind at all. They got paid.

*How much?*

Ten, twenty-five dollars, to move out of that place, for the expenses of moving their buildings. First thing I knew, there was nothing at all. We had a nice school built there, a church, a store, and they had a post office. They had everything. In that school there, we used to play ball, when the people were living there. I felt sorry. I was lost when I got there because the people were gone, and the land was there. And to see that place where we used to live, where we were raised, it was abandoned. Nobody around. Anyway, I left Binscarth and went up to Crane River. My sister was over there.

*Crane River, in Manitoba?*

Yes. I stayed there for the rest of the summer. Then I went to Russell, then to Binscarth. I found my brother, Louis, living on a farmer's land. I stayed there till winter came. Then the war broke out. I went back to Russell and joined the army. I stayed in the army till 1946. Yes, everything was lost cause my place where I was raised was gone. And I couldn't find the people. They were scattered all over the country, in Saskatchewan and Manitoba. Some were in Crane River and some were in Winnipegosis.

*What could have been done for the people?*

Well, if they could have stuck together, like they did in Saskatchewan —stick together, work together— they could have gotten that land back. Free of charge. Then they could have lived there. They could have gotten help, as well as what they get now. See, people are getting welfare now. There's no work. Not like the way it used to be. It's all machine work. They have to support these people with welfare. If they don't support them, these people will starve to death. There's no work. Well, there is work but it's not open to them. They live there, they live here, they live in every town—people in every town, on welfare. The welfare pays for the rent, the Hydro, the water; it supports them with special needs and food. They could have done the same in that place they were in, if they had gotten a reserve. It would have been less expensive for the government to support those people.

*Did you know in 1938, that the Metis people were pushed out of Ste. Madeleine because of the PFRA?*

Yes.

*You knew that. And did you also know that the PFRA applied right across the provinces, from Alberta to Manitoba? It wasn't discriminatory to the Indians or the Metis. It applied to everyone who was on this particular kind of land. Did you know that?*

I didn't know that.

*No one told you that?*

No.

*Were you told that you would get an equivalent amount of land if you paid your taxes on that land? And most of the Metis people who lived in Ste. Madeleine, didn't pay taxes?*

That's right.

*So they had nothing to claim.*

Yes, yes. Nothing to claim.

*So that was the law. That's what the government said. Do you think it was right?*

No. No, because the way I thought about it after I came out of the army and studied the land claims, was that they did what Hitler did to the Jews in Germany. Pushed them out of their homes. If they didn't do this, didn't do that, they'd burn them out. I found that out. If they didn't move their stuff out, if they wanted to stay, their houses would be burned down. They didn't have basements like they have now, they had cellars. They had to close all those cellars and wells, to put the cattle in there, so the cattle wouldn't get hurt. What about the Metis? They got hurt. Cattle couldn't get hurt but the Metis got hurt. That's how they looked at it. They made slaves out of the Metis. In St. Lazare, they made them cut brush and build bridges. My brother, Louis, was working on that. They had to go in the water to build those bridges, in the winter. And they pretty near froze to death, breaking ice and getting them to build those cement forms for the bridge. That's cruelty. That's not helping the people at all. And they made them cut wood. I think it was a dollar and a half a cord.

*Should they compensate the Metis who were there?*

Well, they should. They should.

*What can they do to help all those families who were there? And who should do it? The municipality of Ellice? Or the provincial or the federal government?*

Well, it should be all three of them, together. That's what I figure.

*Do you ever go back to Ste. Madeleine?*

Well, I love going in there. I love to look at that place. It's a lovely place, very very lovely. It's a nice place.

*Do you become emotional when you go there?*

Oh yes.

*What happens to you when you go there?*

Well, I don't know. I get kind of lonesome, wishing to be back again, in that place. Because that's where I was raised. We made our living in there. We had gardens. We had everything we needed there. And another thing: we were raised with a rifle and traps. That was the winter living. We used to kill anything we wanted to eat—rabbits, partridge, jumpers. We lived on that.

Today, there's nothing. There's a lot of people who didn't understand what I said about that. I talked about that at the meetings, about these animals and birds and fish disappearing. From poisoning. All kinds of chemicals they put in all the lakes. All the waters, the rivers, the streams, they're all polluted. Can't use that water, anymore. We used to drink the water out of the sloughs. We used to drink that water—it was clean. From the rivers, streams, and springs, we used to drink all that water. Never used to make us sick.

I worked in 1960, 1962, in Brandon, landscaping and I went down to Minnedosa. Coming back, I was dry. So I went to drink from a nice clean little slough. No bullrushes or nothing, just grass. And I dipped a cupful of water and drank that. Well, I don't know, I got an awful diarrhea. I was sick, very sick on that. I didn't know the water was polluted.

They polluted this country. The air is polluted. The ground is polluted. The trees, the grass, all that grows here is polluted. Because when they spray the fields at night, it evaporates this land to a mess. Like a stream, if a wind comes through, well, that dampness goes up and that stuff is carried into the bush. Don't matter if they didn't spray there. And then the cattle, the wild animals, they eat that. The ground is cooked with chemicals. Well, they've got to eat that, these animals. They've got to drink that water. They're dying off. They have no place, no clean place, to find food to live on. And the muskrat, the ducks, they live in that water. They eat all that and we eat them. The grain, they make flour out of that and make cereal out of that. And we have to eat that. That's why there's so many sicknesses now. Not like the way it used to be before.

This country was beautiful once. Today, there's not much beauty.

Cause back then, you could see, in the spring, around the month of May, you could see all these bushes all white with blooms. Wild fruit, everything, was growing in bloom. Today, you can't see a bush blooming. There's no bush left. It's all dust.

*Harry, if you could live another 83 years, what would you hope that the Metis people would achieve?*

Well, I don't know. Maybe if they could get that place back again, Ste. Madeleine. But it's all torn up; it's polluted. We went over there to pick us some raspberries, strawberries; we couldn't find anything. It's all killed by the cattle. If there were no cattle in there, well, only a certain amount of cattle because we had cattle there, they wouldn't have destroyed everything. There's no more wood. It's all turned to ashes. They turned that bush upside down, putting crops there. Sure, it's a help. It's quite a help. But what about the bush? Where are you going to get the energy? There's no bush. They've got no energy from the bush to help the crops. There used to be a dew at night that came to the woods and the fields. I used to know because I was raised on the farm.

We used to work with horses and one plow. I used to walk behind the harrows all day. We had to get up at four, five in the morning to feed the horses. We combed them and cleaned the barns, took the manure out. Seven o'clock, we were out in the fields, working till six at night. Then we had to feed the horses, go for supper, then back out to comb the horses, bed them and feed them for the night. That was a day's work. That's a lot of work.

Today, they sit in a tractor seat, or car seat, and they call it work. They go out working the fields. It's not them doing the work; it's the tractors working. Now, they take all those jobs away from the people who used to do that work. They put machinery in there. No work for the men. It used to take, oh, I don't know how many, to do the stooking, the thrashing and making hay. Today, one man can make hay. Where's the rest of the helpers? We used to plow four acres a day. If we put up five acres a day, that was a good day's work. There's seeding. We used to do sixteen to twenty acres a day. Today, one man can seed a section a day. But the grain, when we thrashed it, it was rosy, not pale like it is today. No dampness, no bleach. That grain was good grain. That was a reward.

*Harry, did anyone in your family tell you about Louis Riel?*

My grandfather, Edward Pelletier, told me about him. They were sitting there, at a meeting of the Metis. The bishop and the priests were there. It was before the railroads.

Louis Riel said, "I'm going down to the States to get help with this rebellion we're going to have. When I come back here, there'll be no redcoats here. We'll clean them all up!"

Then the Metis said, "No, we're not going to let you go. Let's not let him go. He's going to run away."

Then Louis Riel said, "No. I'm not going to run. You fellows are going to live. I'm going to die. I got to get help. We got to deal with them. It's not us who's going to win the war; it's the other nation. There's truth in what I'm saying."

My grandfather said there was not a wind, not a bit of wind.

Riel said, "The truth I'm going to use, if the good Lord hears me, I want that flag to go with the wind." And that flag opened up just like a big wind. And everywhere else, there was no wind at all.

The Metis asked, "How's it going to happen, this rebellion?"

Louis Riel, standing facing south, said, "On my left side, it's hot; it's burning. But on my right side, it's cold."

Nobody knew what that meant. My grandfather says, "Nobody understood what he was talking about, but the enemy was on his left side and we were on the right side."

So my grandfather told me a lot about Louis Riel and the Metis people and the rebellion.

*Your grandfather was there?*

Yes, oh yes, at the Batoche rebellion. Well, the Indians took all the guns away from these redcoats. They didn't have any guns to use. The Indians brought all the guns down to the Metis camp.

Louis Riel told them, "Take them back. It's not fair. We've got to fight fair. Fair play."

So the Indians took them back. Then they fought. They fought a good fight, I guess. Then they were getting short of ammunition. Then that priest, there, what was his name? The priest there?

*Taché?*

Yes, yes. Then he went and told these other people, fighting the Metis, he says, "Keep on fighting. Don't stop because the Metis have run out of ammunition."

That's when they lost. They looked for Riel after that, chased him around, looking for him. They met him. They didn't recognize him. They had an election, tried to get Louis Riel, if he was there, to sign his name. He wouldn't sign his name and they were yelling, "Louis Riel is here. Anybody see him, let us know."

They didn't know Louis Riel from head to foot. Well, Louis Riel met a redcoat who says, "Louis Riel is here. You know where he is?"

"I don't know. Have you got any chewing tobacco?" Riel asked that police. And the police gave him some chewing tobacco. They were still looking for him. They couldn't find him. He was walking with this kid, a boy, when he met the police, and he says, "Yes I know where he is."

"Where?"

"Right here. I'm Louis Riel." Then they arrested him there. And they took him away.

My grandfather used to tell me a lot about that. Riel's mother-in-law was down here in Ste. Madeleine. See, old Pat Bellehumeur was Louis Riel's brother-in-law. Mrs. Bellehumeur. Yes, that woman died there, that grandmother.

My grandfather, he got shot in the leg, eh. He remembers that. [Laughs] He's got to remember. Ah, there's lots of it. Well, I used to know the Louis Riel song, eh. I don't know if I can sing it. I can't sing. My voice is pretty near gone.

*Well, see what you can do.*

Not now. Maybe some other time.

*Okay. I'll hold you to it. Well, Harry, thank you very much for this extremely informative and moving afternoon.*

150

*HARRY PELLETIER ON HIS WEDDING DAY, 1943*
*Lena Fleury (later Drielick) is Joe Venne's cousin and goddaughter.*

*DECLINE OF STE. MADELEINE, Selby Town, 1940*
*Blind Ambroise Fisher and wife, Véronique (nee) Fleury,*
*with the children of their daughter, Rose.*
*They were one of the dispossessed families resettled in Selby Town,*
*after Ste. Madeleine was made into a community pasture.*

## LENA FLEURY

*Of the five men and women interviewed for this story, Lena Boucher Fleury is the only one who was actually born in Ste. Madeleine, and lived there until 1939, when the Prairie Farm Rehabilitation Act [PFRA] established the pastureland. Her father, Norbert Boucher (son of Hilaire Boucher), was born in Fire Mountain, Saskatchewan, but moved to Ste. Madeleine in 1908, to homestead in the Deer Horn Creek area.*

*Lena, born in 1915, was the oldest of Norbert Boucher and Mary (nee) Fleury's five children. She attended Belliveau School to grade six. In 1937, at age 21, she married Dan Fleury, also from Ste. Madeleine. After the community was disbanded, Lena and her family moved to Saskatchewan, where she began to scrub for farmers, with her husband and her father.*

*Lena and Dan had nine children, five of whom were delivered by Lena's aunt, Véronique Fisher. Eventually, the Fleurys saved enough money to buy 80 acres near Binscarth. When Dan was too sick to farm anymore, they gave it to one of their sons.*

*Lena and Dan now live in Binscarth. She loves playing bingo, socializing with friends, several times a week. If given the choice, Lena would prefer to return to the rustic community life of Ste. Madeleine.*

*Joe Venne joined Lena for her interview.*

*Could I have your name and could you tell me how you did in bingo last night?*

Not too good. [Laughs]

*And your name?*

Lena Fleury.

*Okay Lena. Can I ask you for the name of your father and your mother before she was married?*

Norbert Boucher and Mary Fleury.

*And your grandfather and grandmother on your father's side?*

Hilaire Boucher. I don't remember her name.

*What about on your mother's side? Your grandfather?*

I don't know. He died a long time before she got married. So I never asked her.

*How many children were there in your family?*

Five.

*And what were their names?*

My brother is Hilaire Boucher. And my sisters are Lily, Lucy and Ida. Three sisters and one brother.

*And are they all living?*

No, two of my sisters died. One was 62 and the other was 52.

*And your parents. How long did your parents live?*

Well, my dad died in 1972. My mom died in 1939.

*Did your father remarry?*

No, no.

*Where are your parents buried?*

Across the river over there. In Ste. Madeleine.

*I was there yesterday. Do you have name plates over their graves?*

Just my dad.

*But not your mom. You know where she's buried though?*

Yes, yes.

*Are you going to put something up?*

Yes. Someday.

*How many people do you think are buried there?*

God, I don't know. I can't tell you.

*Can you guess?*

Around 400 or 450, something like that.

*And, if you don't mind my asking, how old are you?*

I'm 71.

*Well, you're just a spring chicken. [Lena Fleury laughs.] After talking to another old-timer, you're just a baby. Where were you born?*

In Ste. Madeleine. We were all born over there.

*What year was that?*

In 1915.

*When did you leave Ste. Madeleine?*

We left there in 1939. The time they started to make a community pasture there.

*Why did you leave?*

Well, we had to. Everybody . . . .

*Who said?*

Everybody went out, so we didn't want to stay there.

*Why did everybody go?*

I don't know. I don't understand why.

*But you left.*

We had to leave, yes. There was nobody around.

*Before you left, what did you live on? Did you have acreage?*

No, we didn't have land. We just stayed there. Some of them, they had land, but not all.

*What did you have? What kind of buildings?*

Log buildings.

*Just one?*

No, two. My dad started building a kitchen but he didn't finish it. We left.

*So you had two log cabins. And who lived in each one?*

Well, one was for the bedroom, one was the kitchen. He was going to make another room.

*Okay. When you left in 1939, do you remember what season?*

It was in spring.

*Where did you go?*

We went to Saskatchewan. Gerald, Saskatchewan.

*And did you have land there? Did you have a house?*

No, no. My husband hired himself out for four years.

*Who gave you a house?*

A farmer. He didn't give it, but he told us to stay there.

*Oh, I see.*

**Joe Venne:** Can I interfere?

*Sure.*

**Joe Venne:** They were living in that house because Dan was working for this farmer already. This farmer gave them lodging while Dan was working for him.

*Sure. Okay. Did he pay your husband as well?*

For what?

*When he was working?*

Yes.

*And did you get any kind of help to move to Saskatchewan?*

No. We had a little car, so we moved with the car.

*What kind of car did you have?*

It was a Ford, a 1926 Ford.

*Really. And your home you had there, what happened to it?*

They burned it down.

*Who were they?*

People from St. Lazare. I don't know. Fouillard, I think. Or else, Selby. I don't know who exactly did it.

*Did you see it being burned?*

No. They burned it after we left.

*Did you want to leave Ste. Madeleine?*

No. I didn't like to leave but my husband had to go out to work. I had to stay home by myself. I didn't like to stay there all by myself.

*Right. So what did your husband do before 1939, in 1937, 1938?*

He was working here and there for farmers. For our living.

*And you came back to Ste. Madeleine to live. Your community?*

Yes.

*And who lived in your house there, just you and your five children?*

No, I had two children at that time.

*Your father didn't live with you?*

He had his own place.

*What did you do for water? Where did you get water?*

We had a well there, not too far from the house.

*Who made the well?*

My dad and Dan, I guess.

*Was the water very deep?*

Fifteen feet deep.

*And can you tell me a little about food. Where did you get food? From the bush at all?*

Sometimes, yes. Chicken. Prairie chicken, rabbit.

*Did you get jumpers?*

Yes. Sometimes.

*Did you shoot? Was it you who went out shooting?*

No, not me. My dad used to go out hunting.

**Joe Venne:** He was one of the best shots in the country.

*I see. Did you have a little ice place to keep your food and your meat?*

No, we just kept them in the well. We put them in the pail . . . .

. . . *and lowered it down. Oh, right. Keep the animals away, and the dogs, I guess. And what other foods did you have besides that?*

Not too much. When my husband was working, he used to bring home a little bit, every Saturday. Flour, tea, sugar.

*Where did he buy it from?*

Here in Binscarth.

*And can you tell me a little about the kind of food you would make? On an ordinary day in Ste. Madeleine, what would a meal consist of?*

Well, We used to make bannock and bread. We cooked some rabbit some time. Make soup out of it. We'd boil it and after, we'd put flour with it.

*Vegetables. Did you use vegetables?*

Well, sometimes, yes. We used to have gardens. Oh yes.

*Oh, you had a garden. What did you grow?*

Potatoes and carrots. Turnips. All kinds. Cucumbers, we used to save for the winter and make pickles with or something.

*Did you take any wild berries from the bushes?*

Yes. Strawberries, raspberries. We used to have lots of strawberries and cranberries.

*What did you do with them? What did you make out of them?*

We made jelly and jam. We put them in the cellar for the winter, you know. We used to pick everything. Try to save for the winter. It was a hard time, at that time.

*What period are you referring to?*

Well, 1930 to 1935, we didn't have much work for the men. We used to dig for the seneca root.

*And what did you do with the seneca root?*

We'd sell them in the store.

*What do they use it for, seneca root?*

I guess they shipped it somewhere, but I don't know where.

*And did you do any trapping?*

No. We didn't trap.

*So it was labour your husband did, that sort of thing.*

Yes.

*You didn't have any farm at all?*

No.

*Just a little garden in the back.*

Yes.

*What was the soil like in the area?*

Well, it was not much over there. Mostly sand. Got to have lots of water to water the ground, if it didn't rain, you know.

*How many people lived in Ste. Madeleine at that time?*

Around 45, at least. Maybe more.

*All together? What year was this?*

Ever since I could remember.

*Okay, now do you remember how long Ste. Madeleine was there? If you were born in 1915, did you father tell you? Was he born there?*

No, he was born in Fire Mountain, Saskatchewan.

*And when did he move to Ste. Madeleine?*

God, I don't know. Before he got married, anyway.

*But you don't know the year he came. Do you have an idea maybe?*

Well, they got married in 1913, so maybe five or six years before that.

*So about 1908?*

He got married with another woman first, a Flammand. And she died. And later, he got married to my mom.

*Were there any children from the first marriage?*

Two. But they died.

*They died. Did you know them?*

No, no.

*They died before you were born.*

That's for sure.

*Okay. This is a question that I've asked Joe, and a question that I wonder if you have an answer to. The community in Ste. Madeleine was known as a Metis community. What does Metis mean to you? How is a Metis person different, if at all, from anybody else?*

I don't know. It's just . . . Metis is mixed somehow. That's why they call them Metis. My grandfather is a Frenchman and he married an Indian. They mixed with a different kind.

*There was a school in Ste. Madeleine. Did you go to it?*

Yes. Belliveau School.

*And how long did you go to Belliveau School?*

I was seven years old when I started. I finished when I was eighteen.

*And what grades did you go to?*

Three to six.

*And did you go every year?*

Yes. No. In winter time, we couldn't go. We didn't have enough clothes to wear sometimes. We had no shoes to go to school in wintertime. We had to stay in. So in springtime, we'd start again and go till fall.

*So who were your teachers? Do you remember?*

My first teacher was Poirier, I think. He was a Frenchman.

*What language did he teach you in?*

English.

*And French?*

No, I never went in French. They used to have French there, half a day. But when I started, they'd already quit that.

*What language did you speak at home?*

French.

*So your first language was French, and then you learned English at school. And who were your other teachers at Belliveau School?*

A Frenchman from St. Lazare. Blouin. That's all.

*Those were your teachers. What was your really good subject?*

Spelling. That's all I know.

*You were a good speller, in English. And did you enjoy school?*

Oh, yeah, that's for sure. But the last teacher that we had was a poor teacher. Mr. Blouin. That's why we didn't learn anything. Sometimes, he would sleep and let the kids play outside all day. [Laughs]

*Did he hit the kids? Did he yell at them?*

No. No.

*What other subjects did you learn, besides spelling?*

Just the regular. I didn't care to go to school with that teacher. I couldn't learn anything. I might as well have stayed home. When the first teacher left, I was in grade six. I went to school with him all the time. I stayed in grade six until I finished.

*If you could have continued school, what would you have done?*

Well, I don't know. At that time, it was not like today, where you can go someplace to be a nurse or teacher or a bookkeeper or something else. I didn't have an education for that. I couldn't go anywhere to learn more. So, I quit, and that's it.

*And how old were you when you got married?*

I was 22.

And was your husband from Ste. Madeleine, too?

Yes. Dan was from Ste. Madeleine, too.

*He was. So did you know him for many years?*

Well, I used to see him once in a while, you know.

*In those days, were the marriages arranged or just between the two people? In other words, did your parents speak with his parents?*

Yes, yes. They used to go and talk to the other people. But Dan had no dad and mother; they died. So, they couldn't speak to anyone.

*But the marriage was approved by your parents?*

Yes.

*As soon as you were married, did you have your own house?*

Yes. We had a little house behind my dad's house.

*What year were you married?*

It must have been 1937.

*Did you have a ceremony?*

No. No, we just had a little meal, you know. Just the close relatives. Not like today.

*Okay, then when you were married, you had a house of your own. Was the house ready before you moved in?*

No. We stayed with my dad for a while and we built a little house there.

*But by this time, in 1937, people were beginning to talk about moving out. So weren't you worried about all that?*

No. We didn't think about it; didn't have it worked out. At the time they moved the people, so we had to move, too.

*Why do you think the Metis people were told to leave Ste. Madeleine?*

I don't know. Because they didn't want those people there, I guess. Metis people were not allowed to stay anyplace. [Laughs]

*So when you moved, what were your feelings?*

Oh, I didn't like to leave that place, you know. We were born there, so we didn't like to leave the church and everything there. Didn't like that, but we had to.

*How did you behave? Did you cry? Did you get upset?*

I never cried. But I didn't like it.

*Did you say anything to anybody? Did you tell anyone that you didn't like it?*

Oh yes, lots of them.

*Who? Who did you talk to?*

I talked to some of them . . . .

*From the community?*

Yes.

*Did anyone from the government, or from the municipality come to you and tell you why you had to go?*

No, they never said anything. They just told us, the people in that place, we're supposed to leave. It was going to become a pasture. They were going to put cattle in there.

*And did you get any money to move out?*

No, we never got anything.

*Did you know some people got money? Did you know that?*

After that, yes. Not right away. I heard that later.

*Before I started these interviews, I did a bit of reading. And I found out a bit about what was happening.*

Yes?

*From what I read, the federal government passed the PFRA, which meant they would make pasturelands, on the prairies. So that it wasn't only the Metis in Ste. Madeleine who lost their land, but it was also people in Alberta, and Saskatchewan. It was done because the land wasn't good for agriculture.*

Oh, I see.

*But what I also found out was that the government had to give an equivalent amount of land. So if you lived on 80 acres of land, they had to give you 80 acres of land somewhere else. But only if you paid your taxes. Did you pay taxes on the land you were on?*

No, no, no, no.

*So is it true to say you were squatting on the land?*

Yes.

*And nobody ever told this to you or your father or your husband?*

No, no, no. We never talked about it.

*What do you think about it now, 48 years later?*

Well, I don't know. I think they should give something to the Metis people.

*What?*

A place. I don't know. They should give a place for us to stay, at least now. After we moved all over the place. It's trouble to move all over. Rent a house . . . .

*A community?*

Yes. They should.

*Should they give the Metis people Ste. Madeleine back again?*

I hope . . . I wouldn't mind it, would you?

*If they did, would you go back?*

Sure. If . . . if everyone else went. [Laughs]

*Do you go back to Ste. Madeleine even now that it's pastureland? To the cemetery and to places where . . . .*

Yes. Sure, I like it over there.

*. . . the old church and the old school were? What feelings do you have when you visit there?*

Oh, when I go back there . . . I don't know. I get happy when I see it.

*Mrs. Fleury, yesterday, I spoke to George Ducharme. We walked all over, in Ste. Madeleine and visited. And he told me about a dream he had of visiting with all the old people from Ste. Madeleine. He felt his dream meant something. Do you ever have dreams and feelings about Ste. Madeleine?*

Before. A long time ago. Now I don't dream anymore. But I used to dream a lot before. Used to dream just like I seen everybody, about people we had, the young ones, all the young people there. We used to play ball on Sundays, you know. We used to have fun there a long time ago. But I don't dream anymore.

*Can you describe Ste. Madeleine as you remember it? Were people good to each other?*

Oh yes, they were good. Got along good down there. Before the war. They never drank like today, you know.

*There was no booze?*

No, no. The young ones, the boys, they never drank. Used to have dances and nobody drank.

*A little home brew? Sometimes?*

Well, just the old people, they used to drink. Like my grandparents. The young ones, they never touched it. We used to have lots of fun. Without booze. [Laughs]

*You had parties?*

Yes.

*Who played . . . .*

We had lots of players, eh?

**Joe Venne:** Even your dad.

Yes, my dad.

*What did he play?*

Oh, reels and waltzes. Jigs.

*The fiddle? He was a fiddler?*

Yes.

*Who else?*

Oh, one of my cousins, Bill Boucher, Jack Boucher. Oh, and his brother, he was a good player. There were lots of players a long time ago. But now you don't have that. Just booze. [Laughs]

*What about singing? Did you sing?*

We used to sing, yes.

*You were a singer?*

Oh, not too much, but I used to sing anyway. [Laughs]

*Okay, we've talked about music, and parties. Was the church an important part of the life of the people in Ste. Madeleine?*

We had church only once a month. We had priests that used to come from St. Lazare.

*And if there were a funeral, would they come in specially?*

Yes. But we never missed a Sunday without a mass. We had to go. Everybody went.

*Now, did people use money, or did they trade with each other? Did you have a lot of cash around?*

Oh no, not very much. Money was scarce at that time. No work, eh. Even the farmers had no money. Sometimes you'd go to work, and get some beef, or pork, something like that. No money. It was hard, you know. My husband used to go thrashing. He'd start early in the morning till late at night, for a dollar a day. That's all we had.

*A dollar a day?*

Yes, a dollar a day. [Laughs]

**Joe Venne:** Thrashing was thirteen hours a day.

*Thirteen hours a day. Was that enough money, a dollar?*

Well, everything was cheap, you know. Tea wasn't even twenty-five cents a pound. Wasn't much for a hundred pound of flour, a dollar and a half. So, if he worked all week, we had enough to buy lots of groceries. [Laughs]

*When you were married, and you were living in Ste. Madeleine, what did you do? If your husband was away working, what did you do with your time? You were at home with the children?*

Yes, yes.

*Did it ever occur to you that maybe you wanted to do something else? Because today, women work and do all kinds of jobs. Did you ever, in those days, feel angry that you were stuck in the house? Or were you happy with your role?*

Oh, I didn't mind, because I knew that there was no work at all for women to do anywhere else. Staying home to look after the kids and clean the house, and wash and cook, I didn't mind that.

*Now, what about medical things? If you had a toothache, in those days, who fixed your teeth?*

Nobody. We didn't have anyplace to go for that. If we had toothaches, well, we just had to stand it. [Laughs]

**Joe Venne:** Your mom was a doctor.

*Your mom was a doctor?*

**Joe Venne:** She had lots of medicine.

Yes, we never went to the hospital. We never went to see a doctor. We used to drink medicine my mom made.

*And did that help?*

Oh yes. That kind of medicine is better than what you take from the hospital or from the doctor now.

*Yesterday, when we were walking in Ste. Madeleine, we were there with George Pelletier, who's only 30, but he used to go with his father, Harry Pelletier. And we were looking at some green plants that were growing there and he said, "That's medicine. My father used to use that, you know." Do you know of any special medicines? Did your mother teach you?*

No. Well, I used to go with her to dig some up, you know. But I don't remember much. There's nothing anymore, anyway. They use all kinds of spray. They kill everything now. You can't dig up anymore medicine. Maybe somewhere you can still get some. I don't know where, though.

*Now then, if you had no doctors and no dentists, who helped to deliver the babies?*

Oh, the old ladies. They used to come.

*Did you have very many women who died in childbirth?*

No, no. I don't remember.

*And was childbirth painful? Did you have a lot of trouble?*

I don't think so.

*Do you remember your own deliveries? Did you have easy deliveries?*

Yes, yes. I never had trouble with my kids. People long ago, I think, were more healthy than now. Gosh, I had five that were born in my home. We never went to the hospital.

*You had help, though, with your deliveries?*

Yes, I had help. I had two in Ste. Madeleine. Then, I had three in Saskatchewan. After that, my husband wanted me to go to the hospital because the old ladies were all gone. Nobody to look after me anymore.

*No midwives?*

No. I had to go to the hospital.

*Now, if I could go back to Ste. Madeleine, how would you spend your day? What time did it usually begin?*

Oh, we used to get up, not too late. But sometimes, when we'd go for a party, we'd sleep late. [Laughs] But we used to get up early, probably it was work time. Early. Not now. It's different now.

*And what was your routine? For instance, did you have diapers for the babies or did you use moss or anything natural?*

We used to buy cloth or something to make diapers. We made their clothes, too. We didn't have too much to buy.

*And did you nurse your babies at the breast most of the time?*

Yes, mostly. I didn't use bottles till the fourth one. I had to give bottles to the last two.

*Did they have wet nurses in Ste. Madeleine? If a mother had no milk, was there another woman who could give milk?*

No, we used cow milk.

*And within Ste. Madeleine, were there some people who had land, like Joe who had 80 acres, and had cows and animals . . . .*

Yes, my uncle, Tom Boucher, had cows, not too far from Ste. Madeleine. We used to get butter and milk from him.

*Do you remember people not getting along with each other in Ste. Madeleine, maybe having an argument or something like that?*

Oh, maybe sometimes. I don't know. I don't remember. I don't think so, eh. Not too much.

*When I spoke to Joe earlier today, one of the things that impressed me was the fact that people helped each other so very much. Everybody was poor.*

That's for sure.

*But if somebody was poorer than somebody else, they would help.
Can you remember any particular time when you helped somebody,
or somebody helped you?*

Well, a long time ago, the people used to build houses with logs, you
know. Everybody would gather and put up the walls. Finish
everything in one day. If somebody else needed a house, well, we'd
go over there, as well. To help each other.

*Lena, as a woman, did you have much contact with surrounding
communities?*

No, no, no. I never went out.

*Did you know many people outside of Ste. Madeleine?*

I don't know. I never went outside there much.

*Do you remember when? Like when you moved to, was it Gerald?*

Well, that time my husband was working there so we moved there
with those white people, you know.

*This was in 1939?*

Yes. He worked there for four years, then we moved to Langenburg.

*In Saskatchewan. So you started to move around?*

Yes. Finally, we had a job scrubbing. So I scrubbed with my husband
and my dad. And dad bought a place there, across the river.

*Where is that place? What's it called?*

**Joe Venne:** There's no place. It's just a farming community, nine
miles west from here.

*Nine miles from Binscarth?*

Yes, close to the Saskatchewan boundary. My dad bought a place
there. So we moved there. We bought some cattle. We keep cattle
there. Finally, my husband saved a little bit of money and we bought
another 80 acres.

*This was down by the Saskatchewan border?*

Yes. Close to there.

**Joe Venne:** But this wasn't in Ste. Madeleine. Remember that.

*Then this was after Ste. Madeleine? So what happened? How come you're not still there?*

Well, we gave that place to one of my sons.

*And does he still have it?*

I don't know. I heard he lost it. I don't know why. Maybe he didn't pay the taxes. We used to pay taxes every year. I had a house there, too. A good house. My dad gave his 80 acres to my oldest son and he sold that place. Now he rents a house in Saskatchewan. He should have kept that place, too. We had 160 acres together. We had cows there, used to milk cows. But my husband didn't feel like doing anything, anymore. Getting old. He was sick so we moved in here. This place belongs to one of my sons. He's in Winnipeg.

*I see. And you're going to stay here, permanently?*

Yes. I wouldn't leave this place . . . . I like this place but there's no waterworks, you know.

*So it's a bit difficult?*

It's hard in wintertime, you know.

*Are you thinking of moving because there's no water here?*

Well, I guess so. I got to move. I don't know. I don't feel like it but I guess I got to move.

*I'm picking up from what you said earlier, that when you grew up in Ste. Madeleine, it was your community. And once you had to move, it's as if you've been pushed around ever since.*

Yeah, right. [Laughs]

*That's what I'm picking up. And you're still looking, in a sense, for a place . . . .*

To stay for good. [Laughs]

*And to be with your people?*

Yes, that's right.

*You feel more comfortable with them?*

Oh yes.

*Do you mix with a lot of Metis people now?*

Oh yes, there are lots of Metis people. I'm always glad to see them.

*And the people from Ste. Madeleine, do you still see a lot of them?*

No, not very much. I don't think there's many living now. I was just a young one, you know.

*Can you tell me what happened to the church? That you had . . . .*

Oh my . . . one of my stupid uncles, he broke it down. [Laughs]

**Joe Venne:** That was her uncle who built a house out of that.

*Your uncle built a house out of it?*

Yes. I was mad when he did that. He made a house for himself.

*You think the church should have remained there?*

Yes. By rights, they shouldn't have touched that church.

*And Belliveau School, I walked over the foundations of it yesterday. But there was nothing there. What happened to it?*

People from St. Lazare, I guess, they came and hauled it away, huh?

**Joe Venne:** Well, LeClerc bought it. One of the LeClercs bought it.

From Lazare.

**Joe Venne:** No, not from Lazare. Down near the corner there.

Oh yeah. It's a shame what they were doing. They burned all the houses; shot all the doggies, see.

*Did you see them shoot dogs?*

Yes. Yes, at my place.

*Who actually did the shooting? Do you remember the man?*

I don't know. A Frenchman from St. Lazare, anyway.

*And he took his gun and he shot your dog?*

Not my dog. My neighbour's dog.

*And were the neighbours around?*

Yes, but they didn't know what they were doing, eh.

*Why did they shoot the dogs?*

I don't know why. Just to make the people mad, I suppose.

*Did any of the people fight back? Did any of the people do anything?*

No. No, they never did anything. Except my dad. He had his gun. He went out and said, "Don't ever touch my dog. If you touch it, you'll be sorry. I'll shoot you." So they never shot our dog. He went away. He went and shot another dog.

*This was in 1939?*

Yes. The people from St. Lazare were mean to those people. They burned everything. Shot their dogs.

**Joe Venne:** They were paid so much a dog, see.

Oh, I never heard anything like that.

**Joe Venne:** Oh, I heard that.

Yeah, I think they did too much to the Metis people. At least, they should have given them a good place where they could stay, after they took the trouble to move out, you know.

*When I spoke to George Ducharme, he said that his father had consulted a lawyer. But the lawyer died before he had a chance to do anything. Do you know if anyone tried to get this problem looked after? Has anyone spoken to the government or anyone else?*

**Joe Venne:** We did, with George's father. We went to see a lawyer by the name of Pratt.

*And did he say you had a good case?*

**Joe Venne:** Yes. But he died.

*So nothing's been done since?*

**Joe Venne:** Nothing's been done since. We never did have enough money to keep going. Transportation . . . it costs money.

I was going to ask you: the people who had the land before, how can they get it back? Like my dad. He had that place, a homestead, you call it. Can the people do anything about it? To get it back? Or lots of people a long time ago; one time they used to have land, you know. They called them homesteads.

*I don't know the answer to that question. I don't know. Maybe some day, we will have an answer. For now, Mrs. Fleury, I would like to thank you for your time.*

Oh, you're welcome.

*NORBERT BOUCHER, age 22*
*Lena Fleury's father*

*L: TOM FLEURY Dan's cousin*
*R: DAN FLEURY, Lena's husband*

*LENA FLEURY (4th from left)*
*with her sisters, her brother and a friend.*

# THE STE. MADELEINE CHURCH

*Mr. Alfred Lemay was one of the earliest homesteaders and it was on his land (Section 32) that the church of Ste. Madeleine was established. The following journal entries, which cover the period from 1911 to 1915, were Mr. Lemay's own account of the building of the church, and of his observations on the relationship between the Ste. Madeleine residents and the parish priest of St. Lazare, Father Lalonde.*

*This document from the Manitoba Provincial Archives was handwritten in French. The following is the English translation.*

This document retells the main events which have happened in Ste. Madeleine concerning the construction of the first chapel as I can certify with proof:

After the first meetings which took place May 2 and June 2, 1911, in the presence of Father Lalonde, it was decided to construct a building with these dimensions: 30 feet in length, 22 feet in width and 12 feet in height. Each man had to bring at least eleven logs to the site at his own expense.

A few supplied more than his share, for one reason or another, while many supplied nothing. After the church reached ten and a half feet in height, there were only two carpenters left on the site. The tools were laid down and it was declared finished on July 11.

During this time, the Father was absent and travelling thoughout Canada. Things remained as they were until September 25, at which time a third meeting was held to discuss the steps which would have to be taken to finish the roof. For my part, I promised boards and lumber. The priest gave us $25 which were part of the gifts he had been given on his trip; contributions from other people amounted to $32.75, bringing the total to $57.75. I hereby attest that this is all the money that was given with the pressing obligation of completing the chapel, since in our district, there is no building large enough to contain more than a third of the population. Also, the decision was made to give fifteen dollars of the fund to Mr. B. Ducharme to put up the rafters and to finish this enterprise by the month of October 1911.

To everyone's displeasure, the roof was too flat and we had to remove the rafters and replace them with the appropriate ones. When the Father saw it, he ordered me to tear it down completely, without a care in the world that we lacked the funds to replace it.

I had already fulfilled my promise to supply lumber and of the $42 which remained of the contributions, I had yet to procure shingles. I asked the priest, "Do you have money for that expense?"

He answered, "I do not have any."

Therefore, everything was left in this state for eight long months, sufficient time, it seems to me, to allow everyone involved to repair the default in the appearance of the building. Yet, more than ever, it was necessary to have that church. The graveyard was open. Already, a first-class service had been given in my poor little lodging which had had the honour of serving as a chapel. The shipment of boards and shingles had dragged on for more than a year and interest in the project was decreasing.

In June 1912, another woman was dying of consumption. I took advantage of this event to ask the people to please help finish the roof. The Father did not hide his disapproval of my suggestion. Since I had no intention of applying for my diploma in Architecture, and found myself in a difficult situation, I had no time to ponder on this problem. We had barely placed the last nail when the body of the deceased was at the door with the funeral party. In spite of everything, everyone was happy to find a shelter.

There was still much to do. After the roofing, the most pressing item was the plastering. I maintained it should be done by laborers. June and July passed with no one showing up. Most of the residents of Ste. Madeleine were absent, being employed in the fields.

About August 10, they all returned for the haying and harvesting of their own crops. I phoned the Father to say the moment was well-chosen if he wanted to come for "filling the cracks" of the chapel. In fact, he arrived the next day when I was very busy with my haying. However, I left it all to harness my carriage and take the priest around the district to gather all the people for a "working bee". It seemed strange to me that the Father appeared to consent only with repugnance. The next morning at mass, he declared that I had imposed a great humiliation on him, engaging him in this project. However, I had overheard him another time, discuss with a certain gentleman that they should take advantage of this time to make walkways through the cemetery.

I must admit that those nice projects did not fit into my plans. There was too much stress on ornamentation when we had so much to finish on the chapel. Fortunately, to my liking, the priest did not show up for the 30 days of the bee which allowed us to do what was the most necessary task—plug the joints. All that was missing were the door, windows and the floor.

Briefly, the church as it was had cost us $137 but I had only $57.75 in the bank. I supplied the rest and we finished the chapel, confident in the promise by the priest of St. Lazare that upon completion, he would come and establish a regular mission. But to my first request to come one Sunday to say mass at Ste. Madeleine, he answered dryly, "No mass. Before that, I must make arrangements with everyone."

I could not complain too much about this as I understood very well that the advantage of having our religious office here required certain conditions. He gave me authorization to make a basket social for the purpose of buying supplies for the inside of the church.

The social took place on November 17. The results gave us $60.25. We installed a good stove and waited to see our priest to give him the remaining $40 which would pay for our altar. Towards the end of that month, there was a marriage in Ste. Madeleine where the people brought the priest against his will. At this visit, he gave us absolutely no encouragement. He only questioned the conditions about which he had spoken to me on the subject of the mission. He allowed himself to make many reproaches and threats, maybe for good reason, but which he didn't explain. Angrily, he left, leaving us with the impression that he had "shaken the dust off his shoes."

On second thought, I admit that I, too, had taken part in the confrontation. At the end of December, he wrote me in a very nice manner that he was ready to come and establish a regular mission. All we had to do was to pick him up. Unfortunately, my confidence in him was already badly shaken when he made these propositions. It was time, however, to give him the chance to assure himself of the dispositions of the others. Taking advantage of the presence of many of us attending the Midnight Mass at St. Lazare, he announced that he was ready to come and establish a regular service in Ste. Madeleine where he would have a Sunday mass once a month. But blame it on indifference or any other reason, which one is free to guess, no one budged.

During the month of February 1913, he wrote to me to come pick up the altar which had been finished. But "a warm cat fears the cold water"; I had already gotten wind that the said altar cost much more that the $40 we had collected at the basket social. To assure myself, I therefore went to the carpenter who told me that the wood alone cost $40 and he charged $30 for his work and that the priest had promised him he would not deliver the altar until he had gotten paid. I let him know that the altar was to my taste except that it might be too big for the chancel of our church and that if the Ste. Madeleine parishioners wanted to take it, I refused to take the responsibility for the debt. The altar was thus placed in the Church of St. Lazare and we were left with nothing.

Our wait for the visit of another priest had stretched out, [*This appears to refer to another priest, superior to Father Lalonde, in the church hierarchy.*] but I wanted to await his counsel before going to reclaim money from Father Lalonde.

Here is the information I thought necessary to explain the part I had taken in the work on the first chapel of Ste. Madeleine. There can be no doubt that I was more of a nuisance than a help. But I believe I have always done my best and I pray to God that he will not hold me responsible.

Alfred Lemay,<br>Ste. Madeleine, May 1913

Postscript:

On March 21, 1914, Ste. Madeleine saw the arrival of the altar and Father Lalonde made the Benediction on March 23. Everyone was well-satisfied except those who perhaps thought it should have been built by the local people—aware of the "taking from the left hand what the right hand had given." The priest was satisfied and announced from the pulpit that he was ready to come and celebrate Holy Mass every Monday morning. I found I would be away from Ste. Madeleine on the days of the postillion.
A.L.

At the beginning of September 1914, I believe the Father Maillard of Wolseley, Saskatchewan, came to give the high mass and it was not to the taste of Father Lalonde who arrived at one o'clock in the afternoon. I gave Father Maillard a report of what had happened concerning Father Lalonde. The good Father Maillard begged me to reconcile and to all the people of the parish, he promised that in the future, things would change. Out of deference to the kind priest, we consented.

On October 25, Father Lalonde came to make arrangements with the parishioners of Ste. Madeleine. His conditions were that if we would pay him ten dollars, pick him up in St. Lazare and return him, he would commit himself to come and say high mass the second Sunday of every month. Seeing that he had made many trips for nothing, we proposed to pay him two dollars more a month if he would come at his own expense and he was very happy to accept our offer. We were 40 families in the district, so at 30 cents each, everyone consented. But I was sure that many would not pay the 30 cents. We asked the priest for permission to make a basket social and pay his salary with the revenue. We had begun to ask for contributions but had trouble collecting $6.40. Therefore, we had to have the basket social.

On December 19, the social was held and the results were $26.05. To pay for the first month, we added $5.60 of the social money and for the second month's contribution of $2.90, we took $9.10 from the basket social money again. The third month, $2.00 was collected and $10 came from the basket social money.

On February 28, 1915, the balance of the money was $1.35 and it was remitted to Father Lalonde. I was finished with that. Afterwards, arrangements were made and adopted. Mr. Alary and Roger Flammand took on the task of undoing everything that had been done. They told the people to pay 25 cents and that they would go and get the priest in St. Lazare. They created a great disturbance as a few paid their 30 cents and others paid 25 cents. When the priest returned, he approved the 25-cent payments. Therefore, it was useless for me to try to do more.

Next, he continued to do the nasty piece of work with his colleagues, who had promised a priest for the Holy Week, but the priest did not appear. On April 24, he came at night saying we would have mass. He returned the morning of April 27, to say mass for his family and announced that on June 27, he would come to say mass in our chapel. Everyone arrived at the chapel, but no priest. Again deceived!

He let it be known by some that he wanted to come on Sunday to set up The Way of the Cross and they would have a nice ceremony. Again, all the people of the village went to the chapel and waited until seven o'clock at night. Still no priest that day. He arrived the next day but no one knew. He had the ceremony with Alary and R. Flammand and a few ladies were present. "Voila!"

On July 22, the good priest Lalonde arrived around nine o'clock at night. Therefore, on July 23, a Low Mass was said. Again, no one was present.

At the present time, I have sacrificed everything for the desires of Father Lalonde who will succeed that nothing will get done in Ste. Madeleine. Many families have left this place from the discouragement of being so ill-served. Ste. Madeleine have pity on us!

*The following is a letter which was also written in the hand of Mr. Alfred Lemay, during the same period as the journal entries.*

**February 2, 1913: We are asking for help.**

**To His Highness Monsignor Langevin**
**Archbishop of St. Boniface**

**Monsignor,**
    We the undersigned residents of the Mission of Ste. Madeleine, Manitoba, humbly beg of you to deign to consider that now that we have constructed, by our own means, a small chapel—very modest it is true but being, nevertheless, able to contain us for all the official religious functions—and to this effect, send us a missionary who is able to speak our Indian languages. There are many people who cannot confess themselves nor understand the French instructions. We also have about 25 children between the ages of six and thirteen who have not had the pleasure of receiving communion. A few of them would not be able to prepare in any other language but their own.
    Father Joseph Chaumont, whom the majority of us have already known for a number of years, and whose zeal and devotions we have appreciated to no end, comes once in a while up to the mission in Elphinstone. Seeing that he has the facility to take the train at Strathclair Station, very close to the station in Binscarth, we have more than once expressed our deep desire to see him come to us and make us participate in the good deeds that are enjoyed by our compatriots of that place *[ie., Elphinstone]*. But in spite of his constant goodwill, he is forced to refuse for lack of authorization.
    This is the authorization, Monsignor, which we solicit of your kindness. Also, your benediction for these and their families.
    Your most undeserving but most devoted sons:

**John Tanner**
**William Fleury**
**Francois Morrisette**
**B. Ducharme**
**C. Ducharme**
**P. Ducharme**
**Philip Ducharme**
**A. Flammand**
**Roger Flammand**

*STE. MADELEINE CHURCH, 1926 - Retreat (six days)*

## LAZARE FOUILLARD - An Outsider's Perspective

*Lazare Fouillard has the reputation for being an incomparable raconteur. At his current farm home, one mile west of St. Lazare, large numbers of friends stop by regularly to enjoy Lazare's wonderful stories. The generous hospitality is augmented by his wife, Rhea (nee: Laroque) who is renowned for being a charming hostess. Lazare and Rhea have been married for 27 years. They eloped on August 27, 1960, and were married in Winnipeg. They have three children, two sons and a daughter.*

*Lazare was born January 3, 1926, in St. Lazare. He is the second son of Benoit Fouillard and Leontine Simard. His schooling was mainly in St. Lazare, followed by four years at St. Boniface College.*

*He spent alternate times at jobs in British Columbia, at the family garage with his father, at Fouillard Implement Exchange in St. Lazare and Frank Clement & Sons in Russell, Manitoba. He is presently working for Crush Rite Concrete.*

*He was able to provide a valuable outsider's point of view and was very candid and open in talking about what he knew of Ste. Madeleine and of the part his father, Ben Fouillard, played.*

*I'm speaking with Lazare Fouillard, the son of Ben Fouillard. Mr. Fouillard, can I begin by asking you what year were you born?*

January 3, 1926. I'm 61 years old.

*Can you tell me of your earliest memories of Ste. Madeleine?*

Well, my memory is that Ste. Madeleine was about the poorest town or settlement around here, back in the '30s. And my father, being a municipal councillor, took care of the relief. And I witnessed some very sad things, like when those people would come into St. Lazare, in the wintertime, with their dogs and sleds and park in front of our house. My dad would go out to them and I was at his side, listening. I was just a kid then.

*About what age?*

About eight. And they were starving. They needed food. And my dad would question them, find out who they were and who their parents were. Finally, he would take out a little piece of paper and write down an order for food at the store. And the food orders in those days were something like three and a half dollars per family. It wasn't very much.

*Was that per week?*

I think so. I think a big family would get maybe eighteen dollars a month and a single man, five dollars a month. And they weren't allowed to have tobacco or sweets. It was strictly necessities like baking powder, lard, butter, very little butter, and flour.

*Do you remember some of the families?*

Oh, I remember the Pelletiers, some Fleurys, the Vermettes, and the Bouchers, but the Bouchers took care of themselves.

*How come?*

Well, he had the post office. He was a non-drinker and he was a heck of a good guy, you know. A good living man. He seemed to get along very well in the '30s. And he took care of the others, too, you know. He and his wife who is still living today.

*Agnes?*

Agnes, yes. They really took care of the people there, when they could. They had cows and I remember my dad saying they used to give milk to the people who needed it. They were good people.

*They would share it without cost.*

Yes, without cost, very much so. Oh, they were good people.

*Who were the doctors at that time?*

At that time, the only doctor I remember is Dr. Edwards.

*What about Dr. Gilbart from Spy Hill?*

Dr. Gilbart? Oh yes I knew him very well. Well, when I knew him he was in his 80s. He was a pioneer doctor. He would have walked fifteen miles to treat somebody for nothing, for no money at all. He had an office above the municipal office, here in St. Lazare, just before the war.

*And what did he look like?*

He was tall and had a little bit of a hunch back. And glasses. He drove a Model A. And once in a while, he'd get a flat tire and he'd drive on it. I used to be around the garage a lot because my dad had the garage. And he used to have flat tires often because during the war, it was hard to get rubber for tires. And he used to run on the rim to the garage and he'd say, "Try and get me fixed up; I want to go home tonight."
  Then he'd go to his office. And he'd charge 50 cents a visit. Other doctors would charge a dollar. And if you didn't have the 50 cents, it didn't matter. Dr. Gilbart didn't mind.  He also fitted people with glasses. If you had trouble with your eyesight, he'd fix you up, too.

*Was he Catholic or Christian?*

I don't know what his religion was. If he wasn't Christian, he acted like one of the best Christians I knew. Oh, he was very good. Dr. Gilbart had a good reputation.

*The reason I mention him is because the Metis from Ste. Madeleine speak very highly of him. He looked after them and he would take nothing from them.*

Money wasn't his problem. He never bothered with money at all. If you paid him, that was okay. That's what I used to hear from all the people.

*What did you have to do with Ste. Madeleine?*

Well, the first time I went there was with my dad. I was around eight or nine. We used to go there and visit, to find out if they were starving or if they were sick, you know. I remember one house, the Pelletiers, I think. It was in the fall and it was cold and there was no floor in the house. There were about five, six kids there and they had no shoes. And my dad called him out to talk to him privately. I was beside my dad and the kids followed their dad out. There was a little bit of snow on the ground and they were standing in the snow with no shoes on. Apparently, it didn't bother them at all, you know. When I was coming back home, I asked my dad, "Did you see those kids there with no shoes on, in the snow?"
And he said, "Yeah, how would you like to be in that shape?"

*What language did your father speak?*

Always French.

*Always French. And the Metis in Ste. Madeleine?*

My dad spoke French to them but they spoke English, too. They spoke English, Cree and French.

*How much education did they have?*

Not very much. They had a good teacher there in Ste. Madeleine. Mr. Blouin. If he was interested in certain kids who were interested in school, he was a good teacher.

*What grade did the school go to?*

I think it just went to eight or nine.

*What language was taught at that school?*

I would imagine English. I don't know.

*What about the church in Ste. Madeleine. Did you go there?*

Yes. When I was about eight to ten, I was the altar boy and I used to go there with Father Halde. He used to say mass there. *[Father Paul Emile Halde was the St. Lazare Parish priest, from 1929 to 1936.]*

*So this was about 1933. And why did you go? Were there no altar boys in Ste. Madeleine?*

Well, when I served mass there, there was one kid who helped me to serve mass. But he started ringing the bell and he wouldn't stop. In those days, you had to ring the bell whenever something happened, like the elevation of the Eucharist, or whatever. I remember Father Halde telling him, "That's enough. That's enough for the bell." I thought it was very funny at the time. He didn't reprimand him or anything but told him very nicely. But the chapel was full. It was always full.

*Could you describe Ste. Madeleine, back then?*

Well, I remember Joe Boucher's post office. All the houses there were log houses with mud in the cracks. I don't remember what was on the roof. Mostly, they looked like one-room houses. They were shacks. They weren't very good buildings, you know. And the church was made out of logs, too. It seems to me it was white.

*What about alcohol? Was Ste. Madeleine known as a place for drink?*

Not any more than any other place. You see, my father, being a Frenchman, you could drink all you wanted, whenever you felt like it. And he never said anything. I don't know if that's good or bad. In our family, we were taught to respect women which I think we did. But we were taught you could drink all you wanted. And so we drank.

*Did you think that there was much drinking in Ste. Madeleine?*

No, I don't think so. No. They were just poor and it was a normal place. There wasn't any more drinking than there was here, or anyplace else. I don't think drinking was an element there.

*As a young boy, did you play with any of the Metis kids?*

Well, of course, we were taught never to discriminate against anybody. But still, we thought the Metis people were a little lower than we were.

*Why? Why was that?*

Well, I guess everybody thought so. But we sure don't think that now! But you know, it was a habit, that if a person were an Indian or a Metis, he wasn't as good as we were.

*Am I correct in assuming your mother tongue was French?*

Yes.

*What would be some of the expressions you would use in those days to call them, to indicate they were lower?*

Well . . . black s. o. b., you know. In French, *maudit peau noir* , which meant black skin. But you know, that was a matter of ignorance. We didn't beat them up or anything. But I think there was a bit of discrimination there, you know. If somebody married a Metis, well, they married into the lower class, eh.

*Did anybody from your family marry a Metis?*

Oh yes, sure. A cousin of mine married one. He married a Metis girl, but not from Ste. Madeleine. She was the best girl you ever saw in your life. Real nice.

*But there was still this attitude?*

Oh yes, at that time. But not today. Today, I've got a boy who I think is going to marry one of them and I'm proud of it. It doesn't matter at all, you know. But in those days, it was something. We would have liked to go out with some Metis girls but we didn't because we thought it was a disgrace. Although they were a hell of a lot better than we were, you know. [Laughs] I think they were.

*I spoke to some of the Metis about common-law marriages. As a Catholic and as someone from this community, do you know if that was frowned upon?*

Well, they were barred from the community. If someone divorced or lived common-law in our town in those days, he might as well leave. He couldn't come to church. He couldn't socialize with anybody. It was a tough life. But that was common all over.

*Was it more common among the Metis?*

I don't know. In those days, if you didn't go to church, if you lived common-law or if you had a kid before marriage, you were barred. You were completely barred from society. Which I'm proud to say, wasn't what my mother taught me. Or my grandmother, especially.

*Tell me about your mother.*

My mother was Leontine Semard and she was half English.

*And your grandmother?*

Gwyer. Sarah Gwyer. She came from England. I think it was Wales. I would say that if you took a vote of all the people who ever came to St. Lazare, and you asked who was the best person who ever came there, they would all say, even the Frenchmen, that Sarah Gwyer was the best woman. She was charitable. And she was a midwife, too.

*To the Metis, as well?*

And the Metis. She never discriminated against anybody.

*Was she a registered midwife?*

No. In England, they accept that. But here, they don't. But in those days, the doctors used to say to my grandmother, go ahead, because it was far from the hospital and everything else. And she was good. She'd do it for nothing.

*And she brought in many Metis?*

Oh, hundreds.

*Do you remember her going into Ste. Madeleine?*

Not Ste. Madeleine, no. But she went all over the place. I remember when she came into town, here, because we used to go see her and take food to her. Sometimes she used to go to a Metis family because a lady was going to have a baby. My mother or my Aunt Helen would give us food to go and take to her because they didn't have anything. And we'd take them food, for our grandmother and for the kids.

*In 1938, they began to fence Ste. Madeleine off, to make it into a community pasture. You would have been eleven or twelve years old at that time. What do you remember?*

Well, I remember it very well because that's the time they started to build the PFRA in St. Lazare. And my dad had the contract to feed the 50 or 60 people who worked for the PFRA, and he got a dollar a day for each one.

*Were these people who your father was feeding, from St. Lazare, from this community?*

Mostly all the community, yes.

*What work did these people do?*

They made the holes for the posts and did the fencing. They had two or three weeks of work. Then they had to leave a chance for somebody else.

*Did the Metis from Ste. Madeleine do work, too?*

Oh . . . I don't know if they were chased out then. What the officials did there in a lot of cases was to give them so much money to go to Winnipegosis and places like that. And then they burned their houses.

*Do you remember that?*

Oh, definitely. I wasn't there when they did that, but after a few years, they came back and told my father they had been thrown out, that they had been chased out of Ste. Madeleine. My dad said, "You know, there are some people I saw today that weren't very happy because they were thrown out of Ste. Madeleine."
  But I don't know who those people were.

*And why were they thrown out?*

Because they needed the land for the PFRA.

*Did they get any compensation?*

If they did, it was very little.

*Are you implying they should have got more?*

Well, yes. But if you go back 40, 50 years, the government threw them out of there because the land was poor, there. It was sandy. They couldn't raise anything, any crops or cattle . . . very little.

*But they had been there since before the turn of the century.*

But in those days, at the turn of the century, they had buffalo, more deer and all that. But after that all dried up, those people were really starving. They were suffering too much there. And the government figured, well, let's get them out of there. Get them to some place else. In Winnipegosis, or some place where they can fish or make a better living for themselves. Schools would be better. Some moved to Binscarth. And they moved them to a little town which they called

Selby Town and Ben's Town, that was my father, or Fouillard Town, whatever they called it.

*Did anybody gain by the Metis being kicked out of Ste. Madeleine?*

No, I don't think so. If you think about it now, eh? They'd have been better off to leave them there. They would have been home. When they die, they still come and get buried there.

*I spoke yesterday to a lady, Josephine Vermette, who was married common-law to Joe Venne. She said, "You know, when they moved us out and we went to Selby Town and Fouillard Town, we called those places that to make fun of Fouillard and Selby. We felt that they were responsible."*
*And that's how those places got their names because they had no names. Were you aware of that story?*

No, I wasn't.

*I wasn't either, until yesterday.*

All I know is that if there was anything done by my father to those people, he sure didn't get paid for it. He did it because he thought that was the best thing to do. One thing my father didn't do, he didn't discriminate. A lot of times, when those people came to our place for relief, he'd say, "Sit down and have supper."
My dad never got a split nickel for any of that work.

*Could all that have happened today?*

No, that wouldn't happen today. You take my dad, he thought that he was obliged to do that work, that he was the only one who could do it well. At that time, he was councillor and the relief man.

*When your dad gave out relief, where did the money come from?*

The Ellice Municipality. And a lot of times, my dad would take the doctor to Ste. Madeleine during the night. He'd get a doctor from Birtle and take him out there to minister to the people there. And I don't think he got paid. I doubt it.

*If you wanted to put your cattle in the community pasture, what would it cost, today?*

I don't know. About $100 a year per head.

*Where does that money go?*

The federal government. No, no, just a minute, the provincial government bought it a few years ago.

*Who did they buy it from and for how much?*

From the municipality of Ellice. I think they paid something like $190,000 for all the land on the north plains, around Ste. Madeleine, and the south plains which is towards Beaver Creek, south of St. Lazare.

*Do you talk to any of the people who lived in Ste. Madeleine?*

Yes, mostly Charlie Vermette. And Joe Venne was one. And I still talk to "The Devil of Madeleine", they used to call him. That's Ralph Fleury. He used to like to fight so they called him that. But Ralph was a good fellow. And I remember Johnny Fleury but then he died. And I used to know the Pelletiers, there. They used to have heavy black beards.

*When I spoke to Harry Pelletier who was one of the few to be in the Second World War, he said, "You talk about the Jews in the Second World War, well, we were the Jews of Canada. They pushed us out of our homes and they burned our houses and shot our dogs."*

Yeah, and that is the truth. They burned their houses. But then, you know why they burned the houses. That was the dirtiest part of the '30s when they did that. Everybody wanted jobs. They wanted the PFRA to bring jobs in.

*Who were they?*

The people around here. They wanted jobs. And the PFRA was going to give us $60,000 which you could say would be about $15 million, $20 million, today.

*Lazare, do you think there was enormous pressure from the people to do this, and that maybe the Metis people of Ste. Madeleine, were looked at as second-class citizens who could be pushed around?*

Oh, I think so, yes.

*Was there that element?*

Oh, I think there was that element that they said, "Let's get them bloody Breeds out of there and have some work. Let's give them a few bucks and chase them out of there.''

*So that was probably true.*

I think so. Yes. I would say it's really true.

*Who were the people saying that?*

Everybody. I think everybody was for that.

*The white people?*

Yes.

*In St. Lazare?*

Oh yes. Probably including my dad and my uncles and all the Englishmen in the municipality and the Frenchmen. They figured, "Let's get them out of there and let's get some work."
 I would say so. But you know, that was the way of thinking then. And today, that wouldn't be the case.

*What should be done today? Should there be compensation? The Japanese are asking for compensation. What do you think? What is the right thing to do?*

Well, if you're going to give compensation, why don't you give compensation to the Acadians, too? [Laughs] If you want to go back 200, 300 years, you could give a lot of compensation, you know. You could give compensation to the people in St. Lazare, too, because we've been pushed around. So, if you want to start that, then you can start the ball rolling and you'd never finish, eh?

*So, there is nothing to be done?*

Well, you've got to look at the times, what was happening then.

*When I spoke to the Metis people who had lived in Ste. Madeleine, there was not one who did not have tears in their eyes. And not one of them, though, felt vengeful. There was no feeling of revenge. What hurt them was the loss of that community, like losing a part of your family.*

Well, the CNR went into Welby and that was mostly a Metis

community. I knew Welby very well, as an adult. I used to go and buy everything in the store there. Today, I'd have a hard time to find out where the town was. It's completely wiped out. And that was done by the CNR.

*Did the people there get a square deal?*

I don't know. There's not too many people talking so they must have had some kind of a good deal.

*Do you ever remember your dad saying, "We're going to get the Breeds out. We're going to get this $60,000?"*

No, definitely not. My dad would never discriminate in that sense. We were taught . . . .

*But he was a politician?*

But it was a way of thinking in those days. It's just like the people who lived common-law or whatever, who were discriminated against. That was the style then. Today, we don't think that way. Nobody thinks that way.

*Sure.*

Things are different, now.

*Lazare Fouillard, this has been a great pleasure. Thank you very much.*

You're welcome. I hope I helped you out in a way.

## THOMAS BERGER - Legal and Historical Perspective

*Thomas Rodney Berger was born on March 23, 1933, in Victoria, British Columbia, the son of Maurice Theodore Berger of Gotheborg, Sweden and Nettie McDonald Berger of Vancouver. Presently, Thomas Berger and his wife live in Vancouver and they have two children.*

*After receiving his law degree in 1956, at the University of British Columbia, he practised law in Vancouver. From 1971 to 1983, Mr. Berger served as Justice of the Supreme Court of B.C. He was chairman of the Royal Commission of Family and Child Law in B.C., in 1973 and 1974. From 1974 to 1977, he served as commissioner of the Mackenzie Pipeline Inquiry. His report,* Northern Frontier, Northern Homeland, *(1977), was an eloquent and convincing argument against the development of a pipeline across the northern Yukon. He succeeded in placing a ten-year moratorium on the pipeline construction in the Mackenzie Valley to permit the settlement of native land claims.*

*Mr. Berger was highly critical of the 1981 federal-provincial accord which attempted to remove aboriginal rights from the constitution. In April 1983, he resigned from the Canadian Judicial Council, in disagreement with their views that judges should not comment on matters of great public concern.*

*In July of 1983, Berger returned to his work on the issues raised by the pipeline inquiry, by heading the Alaska Native Review Commission which investigated the effects of the 1971 Alaska Native Claims Settlement Act.*

*Mr. Berger is unfailing in his support of native rights. He is currently acting as counsel for the Manitoba Metis Federation [MMF] in their struggle to reclaim land promised in the Manitoba Act of 1870. Two lawsuits are now being brought before the federal and provincial courts on behalf of all Metis who claim descent from the original Red River inhabitants of 1870. The Manitoba Act promised that those Metis families, who lived along the Assiniboine and Red Rivers, would be able to keep their river property. In addition, the children and grandchildren of these families were to receive another 1.4 million acres of land. These promises were never kept.*

*If Mr. Berger wins these two claims on behalf of the MMF, then negotiations for compensation may begin between the MMF, and the provincial and federal governments. At that point, individual Metis communities will become involved in deciding the forms of compensation. Of course, it will not be possible to return land which is now in the hands of private owners. But land which is available and suitable to the individual communities will be one option available. The compensation may take other forms, such as economic development projects, work training or educational programs.*

*Mr Berger has been a guiding light in the legal proceedings of the Metis. As Yvon Dumont, president of the MMF, has commented: "If it hadn't been for Tom Berger, I don't think our case would be going anywhere. He is working on the basis of not knowing exactly when and how we're going to pay him but, nevertheless, believes in the case enough to move ahead with it. As far as we're concerned, he is the best native rights lawyer in the world!"*

*Mr. Berger, there are some critics of the legal claims now being filed, who say that they only apply to those people of Indian and French descent. In Manitoba, will this be a legal fight for all Metis or only those of French and Indian heritage?*

The two lawsuits are on behalf of all of the Metis. Back in 1870, when the Manitoba Act was passed, the Metis were to receive land. The families, who lived along the Red and Assiniboine Rivers, were to be able to keep their lots, and the children of those families, who were called half-breeds in those days, were to receive 1.4 million acres. Thus there would be land for future generations of Metis.

The Manitoba Act applied to everyone of mixed blood who was understood to be a half-breed in those days. And so the two lawsuits are being brought on behalf of all the Metis who claim descent from the people who lived at Red River in 1870. That includes the descendants of the French and the Indians, the Scots and the Indians, and others of mixed Indian descent.

And it includes not only the Metis living in Manitoba, but Metis across the prairies. The claim is being made because the government of Canada and the government of Manitoba did not live up to the promises, made in the Manitoba Act, that the Metis were to get land. Because they never did get the land they were promised, they left the Red River and were dispersed across the prairies.

So the claim is being brought on behalf of all those people.

*Can you give me a rundown of the Manitoba Act?*

Well, as you know, 1870 is the crossroads of Canadian history. Canada was established in 1867 and until 1870, it was a country that comprised Ontario, Quebec, New Brunswick and Nova Scotia. Then in 1870, Canada acquired the great Northwest. This included what are now the prairie provinces, the Northwest Territories and the Yukon. Now that's a gigantic acquisition of land for any country. And in order to persuade Great Britian to let Canada have all that land, Canada made certain promises.

Now there had been an uprising at Red River where the Metis, led by Louis Riel, formed a provisional government. Delegates of that provisional government went to Ottawa, to negotiate with John A. Macdonald, the first prime minister of Canada, and George Etienne Cartier, and they worked out a deal. And the deal was designed to protect everybody here at Red River in what was later to be in Manitoba.

There were to be two official languages, English and French. The schools of the Protestants and the Catholics were to be maintained out of public funds. And the Metis, who knew there was going to be a wave of white settlement coming into the Northwest, into the Red River, once Canada acquired this vast area, wanted guarantees for their land, the land they held, the river lots, and for the future generations of Metis who would come along.

Now all of that was in the deal. What happened was that the parliament of Canada passed an act called the Manitoba Act which incorporated all of these arrangements. The Manitoba Act, since 1870, has been as much a part of the constitution of Canada as the Charter of Rights is today.

So, the rights that the Catholics had to their schools, under the Manitoba Act, were constitutional rights; the rights that the Franco-Manitobans had were constitutional rights; and the rights that the Metis had were constitutional rights. Now, in Manitoba, you have spent the last ten years litigating the question of the rights of the Franco-Manitobans. It was only in June 1985, that the Supreme Court of Canada finally settled the question by saying that when the Manitoba Act provided that there would be two official languages in Manitoba, English and French, this was binding on Canada and on Manitoba. Nothing the parliament of Canada did, nothing that the legislature of Manitoba did, could take away the rights of the French-speaking population of Manitoba, even today, in our own time. French should be treated as one of the official languages of Manitoba.

Now, in the claims of the Metis, we are bringing forth these two lawsuits based on the Manitoba Act, based on the fact that the Manitoba Act is part of the constitution of Canada. And we will ask the courts to say that, just as the parliament of Canada and the legislature of Manitoba had no right, no power to take away the status of French as an official language, because it was entrenched in the Manitoba Act, the parliament of Canada and the legislature of Manitoba had no right to pass laws designed to make sure that the Metis, back in the 1870s and the 1880s, didn't get the land that they were supposed to get. And those provisions of the Manitoba Act—that said the Metis were to get their lots along the rivers, and in addition, were to get 1.4 million acres of land for their children and future generations—are still binding on Canada and on Manitoba, today. That's what the two lawsuits are about.

And the Manitoba Act and the guarantees that it contained are kind of a microcosm of the debates we've had in Canada ever since—the debates between Protestants and Catholics over public funding for their schools; the debates between the English and the French over the rights of the linguistic minorities in each province; and the debates over the rights of the aboriginal people, of whom the Metis are one along with the Indians and the Inuit, and their land claims.

So that's what it's all about. That's kind of a long-winded way of putting it, but it's trying to roll up 116 years of history in a few paragraphs. It's the best I can do.

*Why didn't they get this land, the 1.4 million acres of land, these river lots?*

Well, the argument of the Metis is that it's up to the courts to decide whether this argument is sound. The argument is that the government of Canada decided that even though it had promised 1.4 million acres to the Metis, even though it had promised they would get their river lots where they had always lived, John A. Macdonald, the prime minister of Canada, decided he didn't want to leave this new province, Manitoba, with all of this valuable land, in the hands of the Metis, in the hands of the half-breeds.

John A. Macdonald's private correspondence indicates that he said: "I had to agree to all these things to make sure Riel and the Metis would lay down their arms, so that we could acquire this great, new land."

In his private correspondence which is now in the archives in Ottawa, he said, "But, we are going to try to get out of those promises because we want a lot of good farmers from Ontario to move west to Manitoba. And I want to make sure that they get that land. I don't want the half-breeds to have that land. Even though, under the constitution of Canada, the half-breeds, the Metis were entitled to that land."

Now if promises mean anything, if the law means anything, if constitutions are more than just pieces of paper that you can tear up, whenever you feel like it, then the Metis have certain land rights. They didn't get that land. The evidence shows that only about ten or fifteen percent of the Metis actually got to keep the land they were supposed to get. The rest didn't get their land. And weary, and broken-hearted and without any land, without opportunity to secure a place in the new society that was being established here, they moved west, into Saskatchewan. And of course, the settlers and the government of Canada caught up with them again, fifteen years later, in 1885. And you had the Northwest Rebellion.

But it's not just ancient history. And it's not just curiosity. The Metis are still here, and they still insist on their rights under the Manitoba Act. And what we are doing is going to the courts and saying: "Here are these constitutional instruments and the Metis have certain rights under them. And they never did get this land. Now we want you, the judges, to decide what does all of this mean, today in 1986 and 1987. What does it mean today?"

We say it means they are entitled to their land today. That means if we are successful—and of course, it's up to the courts to decide—the government of Canada and the government of Manitoba will have to sit down and work out a land claims agreement with the Metis. And once we've done that, we will have completed the unfinished business of 1870. You can't escape from your own history. You can't say, "Well that's something we did to those people a long time ago. And we're very sorry about it but let's get on with life."

I mean you can't just sweep everything under the rug. We made promises: I didn't make this promise; you didn't make this promise; Canada made this promise and Canada's still here, and the Metis are still here. And the Metis say that the promise can and ought to be fulfilled today.

*In what way?*

Well, I think they're entitled to the land. They say this means the government of Canada, and the government of Manitoba should sit down with the Metis and work out a scheme so they can get their land. They won't say, "We're entitled to downtown Winnipeg."

The land, true enough, is downtown Winnipeg, but it has been transferred again and again, and has gone through many hands and is now in the ownership of innocent third parties. And one of the things the Metis concede is that they can't take anybody's home or anybody's farm and say, "That belongs to us."

So this is something that has to be worked out carefully, if we succeed. If the courts decide in our favor, it is something that has to be worked out very carefully with the government of Manitoba. It's unfinished business and the sooner it's tackled the better.

*Who is responsible for the Manitoba Act today? Where does it lie? In the provincial or federal jurisdiction?*

Oh, it doesn't lie in the jurisdiction of either the federal or the provincial government because it is part of the constitution. That means that if you have rights under the constitution, if you have rights under the Manitoba Act, they can't be taken away by the federal government or by the provincial government. That's the whole point of the two lawsuits.

*What does the current provincial government in Manitoba say? You've spoken to the Attorney General here. What is their position?*

Well, the government of Manitoba is fighting the case, on behalf of the province. The government of Canada is fighting the case on behalf of Canada. And we're going to court. We're going to fight this out and see if the Metis have a good case. The Metis think they have a good case and we wouldn't be going to court with it if we didn't think it was a case that the courts ought to consider. And I'm sure the courts will consider it. And give it the most serious consideration.

Nobody can be certain of the outcome. But we will do our best to win the case. The government of Manitoba will do its best to resist the claim we are making. The government of Canada will do its best to resist the claim. If, however, we are successful, I am sure that both the government of Canada, and the government of Manitoba, will sit down and negotiate the settlement. They'll have to.

*Why is the current government in Manitoba resisting? What does Attorney General Roland Penner say?*

Well, when I've spoken to Mr. Penner, I haven't asked why he is fighting the case. Those are political decisions for Mr. Penner, as Attorney General, and his colleagues to make. In the same way, I haven't marched into John Crosbie's office in Ottawa and said, "Why are you fighting the case?" That's a decision he makes. [John Crosbie was federal Minister of Indian Affairs at the time of this interview.]

What I have been talking to Mr. Penner about, and the lawyers in his department, as well as the lawyers in the Department of Justice in Ottawa, is about cooperating to make sure we can get the two lawsuits brought before the courts, as soon as possible, so there aren't a lot of technical objections, so that we don't waste time on a lot of extraneous disputes. And we have already had a number of meetings with the lawyers for Canada and for Manitoba to work out in a cooperative way, the most expeditious means of bringing the case before the courts.

But they're still fighting the case; that's their prerogative. They make these choices; I don't. You'd have to ask them why they're fighting the case.

*But why do you think they're fighting it? We're talking of a New Democratic government which has had a more enviable record in its treatment of the native people than the previous governments, and I'm confused by a socialist government not sticking up for the rights of the Metis people.*

Well that's their business. I suppose they discovered in the early '80s when they tried to entrench the rights of Franco-Manitobans, there was a lot of resistance among the people of Manitoba and it may be that they feel if they go to court, fight it out, and if the courts decide in favor of the Metis, then everyone will understand. Then, we have no choice but to sit down and negotiate with them. Now, I don't know what their attitude is based on, but that might well be the basis for their attitude.

I think that the government of Manitoba is certainly putting everything it's got into fighting this case. There's no doubt about that. And that's their right. They represent all the people of Manitoba. They know that there's a certain resistance among the populace here in Manitoba to carrying out the obligations that were assumed under the Manitoba Act. Well, if that means we have to go to court and get the courts to declare what those obligations are, so be it. That was the case with the Franco-Manitobans.

*Can I move this discussion beyond this specific issue? From my own knowledge and experience, I could say that the Metis people are second- or third-class citizens in Canada. Certainly by the standards of UNESCO in terms of economics and education, the Metis and a lot of native people, are treated as less than first-class citizens. I am wondering whether this issue might be addressed, not in your terms specifically with this claim, but in the wider sense, of trying to make all Canadians equal, including the Metis and the other aboriginal peoples. Let's say you win the claim, and they get land and money, compensational and educational trusts; is the bottom line, to give them equal opportunity?*

Well, that may be part of the fallout from the claim, sure. I think the Metis want to advance their position in Canadian society. I don't think anyone would argue with what you say, that in terms of income and education, they are very close to the bottom of the ladder.

But these lawsuits are to enforce promises made to the Metis over a century ago. It seems to me that fundamental to acknowledging the legitimacy of the place of the Metis or any other aboriginal people, or anybody, in our society, is acknowledging that when you write things in the constitution and you say these rights belong to the Metis, or the Indians or the Inuit, or to anybody else, that it means what it says and you've got to live up to those arrangements.

Otherwise, you don't have the rule of law. Constitutions are just pieces of paper the governments can ignore whenever the majority says, well, they think it's inconvenient to live up to those agreements we agreed upon a hundred years ago. I think if Canadians really stand back and think about it, they don't really want Canada to be that kind of country. You know, it's not as if these promises are promises that can't be kept today with good will on both sides, with thoughtfulness and with imagination. They can be.

*A growing number of Canadian native scholars and academics see the land claims issue in terms of capitalism versus communism. They say that the native people can never get a square deal where land is privately held. What do you think, is there merit in this argument?*

That takes in a lot of territory.

The capitalist systems and the communist systems are very much alike in their attitudes towards minorities. Both systems believe in the technological and industrial definition of progress; they believe in assimilating. The whole tendency is towards assimilation of minorities. Communist countries have certainly not been any more prepared than we have been to acknowledge the rights of indigenous peoples, people like the Indians, and the Inuit, and the Metis.

My father came from Sweden and I've been to Sweden. The Laplanders, who are the native people of Sweden and who live in the north, are struggling for exactly the same rights as the Metis are seeking in Manitoba today—for a measure of self-government and for land rights.

So all these Western economic systems, whether they call themselves capitalist or communist, have very much a uniform attitude towards indigenous peoples, the people who were here first. They are reluctant to acknowledge the rights of those people.

In Manitoba, what is quite remarkable is that in 1870, in order to acquire the land and get the Metis to lay down their arms, Canada agreed: "Yes, you folks, you half-breeds living along the Red and Assiniboine, you can keep your river lots. And in addition, we will give 1.4 million acres for your children, your grandchildren and your great-grandchildren."

Those promises were never kept. And my job is to try to persuade the courts. It's up to the courts to decide that those promises are promises entrenched in the constitution that must be fulfilled today.

*Okay. I've been talking with people who once lived in Ste. Madeleine, and I've realized how important that community was to their way of life. Although whole families would leave for months at a time, to work on farms, scrubbing, cutting wood, digging seneca root, they would always return to their own land and log houses in Ste. Madeleine. That was home to them.*

*Whether or not they had paid their taxes, they still would have been forced to relocate, and the community of Ste. Madeleine would still have been lost.*

*And then I asked the question time and again: "Who is the bad guy in this business, in Ste. Madeleine? Who's the good guy?"*

*Nobody pointed a finger: "Well, we didn't pay our taxes. We were squatters." They recognized that. But they said, "They could have treated us better. They could have treated us differently."*

*Many of the people still long for a community of their own, where there is a spirit of sharing, where they have control over their own lives.*

*For example, Lena Fleury, a lady who was born, raised and married in Ste. Madeleine, asked me this question: "Can the people, who once had homesteads there, get that land back? Can the people do anything about it?"*

*So I suppose my question is really to discuss the people themselves, and what this claim means to their soul, to their dignity.*

Well I've found that land claims mean a lot to indigenous people, in every country, because it's a way of asserting the legitimacy of their way of life and their history. In contemporary terms, it's a way of saying to the rest of us: "Look, we have our own history; we have our own way of life. It has changed and evolved over the years. But it is still distinct. And there has to be a place for our history and our way of life today, in Manitoba, in Canada, in the world." And I think that land claims are important to the Metis and to the other indigenous peoples because it is a way of asserting who they are and what they are in the 1980's. And so I don't think we can underestimate the importance of these claims.

*By the way, what brought you to Winnipeg yesterday?*

Oh, I had a meeting with the lawyers for the Government of Canada and the lawyers for the Government of Manitoba. We had a day-long meeting to go over some of the details of the two lawsuits.

*Is there anything about your meeting that is newsworthy, that can be reported?*

No, nothing. [Laughs]

*Well, Mr. Berger, thank you.*

*LOUIS RIEL'S RELATIVES*
St. Lazare, circa 1907
L-R: (Standing) Francis Bellehumeur, Pat Bellehumeur (brothers)
(Sitting) Mrs. Francis Bellehumeur, nee Bernadette Landry; Mrs. Pat Bellehumeur,
nee Cecile Fleury; with son, Victor Bellehumeur
Francis and Pat Bellehumeur were brothers-in-law to Louis Riel.
Pat Bellehumeur helped raise Joe Venne, and taught him the Louis Riel song.
Bernadette and Francis Bellehumeur died in the flu epidemic of 1918.
[Bellehumeur was the original spelling, but it was often spelled as Belhumeur.]

**LOUIS RIEL SONG**
*(Translated to English by Joe Venne)*
*In the battlefield, it's a crime and it's delirious.*
*But I received a letter from my dear mother.*
*I had neither pen, nor ink, but was able to write.*
*I took a knife and dipped it in my blood and wrote a letter to my dear mother.*
*When she received this letter, all written in blood, she said to her children:*
*"Let us pray, my dear children.*
*Let us pray for your dear brother who's in this regiment."*
*Goodbye, mother. We know what it is to die.*
*We will all die in turn.*
*So I am going to die bravely, as we will all have to die, someday.*

## *ABOUT THE AUTHORS*

*Ken Zeilig was born in St. Boniface, Manitoba, and was educated in Manitoba in the '50s, at St. John's Tech and United College, where he studied Arts. His artistic talent found fulfillment in London, England, in 1966, where he pursued post-graduate film studies at Hornsey College of Art and the University of London. Ken has spent 20 years as a journalist, radio broadcaster and television producer, working for Rediffusion Television and BBC in England and CBC in Canada.*

*Victoria Rieber Zeilig was born in Los Angeles, and earned her B.A. in History and M.A. in Folklore & Mythology at the University of California, Los Angeles (UCLA). Her work as a community health researcher in New Mexico, among the Navajo and Hopi people, heightened her interest in native history and affairs. In another career direction, she worked six years as a market research analyst for a Los Angeles advertising agency.*

*Ken and Victoria lived in La Ronge, Saskatchewan for fifteen months, where Ken was a radio producer for CBC. They travelled throughout the north, visiting many Native and Metis communities. They currently live in Winnipeg, where they are engaged on their next writing project.*